THE GENE POLICE

CHRISTOPHER HOLMES NIXON

"The Gene Police" Copyright © 2015 Christopher Holmes Nixon

Canadian Intellectual Property Office Reference: 1122813

Hardcopy Edition ISBN: 978-0-9948128-0-3

Digital Edition ISBN: 978-0-9948128-1-0

Cover Art by Jelena Gajic

Copy Editing and Proofreading by Writer's Digest at www.writersdigestshop.com

Type Setting and Distribution by Book Baby at www.bookbaby.com

Produced by Foehammer Publications at www.foehammerpublications.com

"The Gene Police" is entirely a work of fiction. Any resemblance to actual persons, living or dead, is entirely coincidental.

THE GENE POLICE

Christopher Holmes Nixon

"For he is the minister of God to thee for good. But if thou do which is evil, be afraid; for he bearth not the sword in vain; for he is the minister of God, a revenger to execute wrath upon him that doeth evil."

- Romans 13:4

One

"Central, this is one one, hasty rules of engagement request to follow, acknowledge."

"Acknowledged one one, send roereq when ready, over."

The man in the black suit and tie stared forward from the back of the bus. Overdressed for public transportation and wearing dark form fitting sunglasses despite the darkness, the man restrained his movement to avoid drawing any further attention to himself. Leaning back into the clean but cheaply constructed plastic bench seat, the man in the black suit glanced up along the aisle.

Reclining in the middle of the bus with his arms outstretched along the adjoining seats was a man dressed in an ostentatious tailored pin striped suit worn under a dark brown leather trench coat. The man was speaking in loud boisterous tones which drowned out the ambient noise of the moving bus, arching his head back to expose his shiny crooked teeth in an attempt to entice his companions to laugh along with his incoherent personal narrative.

Reaching up to touch the earbud delicately placed into his right ear, the man in the black suit continued to speak in low focused tones, angling his voice down towards the floor of the bus.

"Para alpha, one times person of interest, male, approximately thirty years of age," whispered the man in the black suit. "Pattern of life indicates a likely affiliation with organized crime."

"Central acknowledges," responded the calm female voice. "Send."

The man in the black suit shifted his attention to the front of the bus, noting the digital roll sign located above the bus driver before turning to look out the window and examine the passing surroundings.

"Para bravo, public bus number one zero three, currently heading east towards the downtown core," continued the man in the black suit and tie.

"Acknowledged, one one," answered the woman. "Send."

The man in the black suit turned back towards the interior of the bus and studied the entourage seated to his front. Sheltered under the left arm of the man in the brown leather trench coat was a woman dressed in a dark fur coat covering an exceptionally short black dress. She was adorned with multiple rings, bracelets, and a number of gaudy gold earrings, and despite the audacity of the man she was with, the woman seemed disinterested in the conversation and divided her attention between her fingernails and a pink cellular phone. Seated to the right of the man in the trench coat and to the immediate left of the woman were two extremely large and physically intimidating men. The two men were dressed in dark pressed suits layered underneath thick leather jackets, both dressed identically as if in uniform despite their civilian attire. The two men rarely spoke, seated upright and smiling periodically in a hollow attempt to feign interest in the endless torrent of obnoxious anecdotes emanating from the man in the leather trench coat.

"Para charlie, two escorts, possibly armed, and one female companion," spoke the man in the black suit.

"Central acknowledges," replied the female voice. "Send."

Glancing to the left and then over to his right, the man in the black suit surveyed the remaining occupants of the bus.

"Para delta, twelve civilians, including the driver," continued the man in the black suit.

"Acknowledged, one one," responded the woman. "Send."

The man in the black suit returned his attention to the unruly man in the brown trench coat. Subtly reaching over to his opposing wrist, the man in the black suit keyed his watch three times in rapid succession as a faint wave of light pulsed across the lens of his sunglasses.

"Para echo, no further info, digital image check incoming," spoke the man in the black suit. "Roereq ends, over."

"Central acknowledges all, image check received, hasty roereq in process," answered the woman. "Wait out."

The man in the black suit placed his hands on his knees and slowly exhaled as the verbal tirade resonating from the center of the bus continued. Approximately sixty seconds elapsed before the speaker bud embedded into the man's ear erupted and the disembodied female voice continued to speak.

"One one, this is central, message, over," spoke the woman.

"Send," answered the man in the black suit.

"Positive return from the image check cross referenced against our database, subject's name is Ryan Polowski," spoke the female voice, speaking swiftly but decisively. "Listed convictions include one count of possession of contraband, two counts of armed robbery, one count of assault, two counts of extortion, background history indicates no children, no recorded social contributions, no political affiliations or charitable donations, estimated income is between figures seventy five and one hundred thousand, no recorded tax deductions in the last four years, and link analysis from the intelligence cell indicates an affiliation with a known crime syndicate, more to follow, wait."

The man in the black suit remained still and static filled his ear as the soft placid tone of the female operator was abruptly replaced by a forceful but controlled deep male voice.

"One one, this is niner, Ryan Polowski is low-level management for a syndicate operating out of the downtown core, this guy is relatively small time and trying to make a name for himself by working his way up the organized crime chain, the irony being that despite his alleged reputation he's still riding the bus like everyone else," spoke the harsh male voice. "Make no mistake, he's a violent little social parasite so it's a good catch nonetheless, hasty roereq authorized as of time now and extant until the target has been prosecuted, minimize collateral damage, escape and evade if necessary, notify this call sign when complete... for the good of all mankind, central out."

The man in the black suit removed his sunglasses, placing them inside his jacket pocket before standing up from his seat and advancing down the aisle.

"Ryan Polowski," spoke the man in the black suit.

The man in the brown leather trench coat, the woman in the tight black dress, and the two large men halted their turbulent verbal revelry to simultaneously look up towards the man in the black suit.

"Ryan Polowski," repeated the man in the black suit, his hands remaining at his sides despite the shifting momentum of the speeding bus.

"No one calls me that anymore," responded Ryan Polowski, snarling to reveal his crooked entangled teeth. "Who the hell do you think you are?"

"My name is Mister Smith," answered the man in the black suit. "Please come with me at the next stop... I have a matter to discuss with you."

"Do you know who I am!" yelled Ryan Polowski, his eyes widening in exasperation.

"I know who you are, Mister Polowski," responded Mr. Smith. "Now please, come with me."

"I'm gonna strangle you with your own tie," said Ryan Polowski, leaning forward in his seat. "Brett, Rock... teach this overdressed punk some manners."

"They never listen," said Mr. Smith.

The two men positioned on either side of Ryan Polowski paused to look over at each other before turning their attention towards the man in the black suit and rising up from their seat in unison. The narrow aisle of the bus canalized the two men into a single file, and the lead heavy set man smiled down at Mr. Smith before suddenly lunging forward.

The oppressive man charged with his arms extended, the palms of his thick hands aimed at Mr. Smith's throat. Raising his hands together in front of his body and placing his right foot to the rear for balance, Mr. Smith reached between his assailant's outstretched arms and gently parted the man's hands outward and away from their intended target. Defeating the incoming attack, Mr. Smith crouched downward, drawing his arms inward and then jetting forward to ram his fists into his attacker's rib cage. Overcome with abrupt pain, the large man winced and involuntarily heaved forward. Mr. Smith reached out and grabbed his stunned opponent by the hair with his left hand while drawing the palm of his right hand back to a ninety degree angle with the rest of his arm. Two cylindrical barbed probes extended from underneath Mr. Smith's suit cuff as he drove his palm into his adversary's neck causing the heavy set man to jar his head backwards and emanate a silent scream of pain. Mr. Smith retained his grip as the man's eyes glared mindlessly upwards and his hulking arms convulsed before releasing his hold and allowing his oversized opponent to collapse unconscious into a twisted pile of appendages.

"Holy...," yelled Ryan Polowski, his shout cut off by the sound of screeching brakes rising up from the floor.

The occupants of the bus lurched forward as the vehicle forcibly decelerated, and Mr. Smith watched as the driver rose up from his seat to tear at the release lever for the hydraulically operated doors. The front door to the bus split open, and a panicked mass surged towards the exit as the remaining passengers attempted to rapidly distance themselves from the violent altercation.

Seated in his original position, Ryan Polowski immediately looked up towards his remaining escort.

"Rock!" ordered Ryan Polowski, the sound of audible fear impacting his speech. "Get this guy!"

The remaining body guard stepped forward in front of his principal, clenched his fists, and then cracked his neck to one side as he stared back at Mr. Smith.

"So you're Rock?" questioned Mr. Smith, stepping over the jumbled figure lying along the aisle of the bus. "That means that must have been Brett who just introduced himself."

The man responded to the comment by exhaling a guttural roar and charging heedlessly forward with a wide left hook. Pausing until his attacker was within striking distance, Mr. Smith crouched forward as the incoming strike surged over the back of his head. Mr. Smith snapped back to a standing position and watched as his opponent, realizing that his attack had failed, rotated his torso in the opposite direction and reached out with his clenched fist for a subsequent assault. Raising his left arm to sharply intercept the incoming strike, Mr. Smith reached down with his right hand to withdraw a short metallic rod attached to his belt and grasped the bar tightly. The cylindrical rod instantly quadrupled in size as Mr. Smith arced his arm upwards to strike the body guard callously in the jaw with the end of the baton. The brutish man fell backwards and withdrew his hands inwards to grasp at the source of the pain, and Mr. Smith surged forward to slam his opponent with his left hand as he raised the baton above his head with his right. Hammering his falling adversary, Mr. Smith continued with a blinding series of strikes until the drumming sound of the heavy set body guard colliding with the plastic floor signalled that the man would offer no further resistance.

Toggling a small switch on the baton with his thumb, the telescopic club collapsed and Mr. Smith returned the weapon to the holster on his belt. Taking a moment to straighten his tie, Mr. Smith turned to face his original target.

"Ryan Polowski," spoke Mr. Smith.

Still slouched along the bench seat of the bus, Ryan Polowski looked down at the floor towards the motionless figures of his body guards, then over to his screaming female companion recoiled in the adjacent seat, and then finally back up to the man in the black suit.

"Who... who are you, man?" stuttered Ryan Polowski.

Mr. Smith advanced forward and watched as Ryan Polowski attempted to push himself backwards through the wall of the bus before reaching into his trench coat to draw a short barrelled chrome plated revolver. Recognizing the contentious movement, Mr. Smith bounded forward and reached out with an overhand grasp to seize the barrel of the gun, twisting the pistol away from Ryan Polowski's hand and tossing the revolver over the back of his head. With a sharp exhale, Mr. Smith lifted his left leg and rammed his foot into Ryan Polowski's throat, pinning his target to the seat with his heel. Mr. Smith reached into his suit, drew out an oversized black 0.44 caliber pistol, and then pointed the weapon directly towards Ryan Polowski's face.

"RYAN POLOWSKI!" yelled Mr. Smith. "You've been tried under article zero zero one of the GENEPOL charter!"

Ryan Polowski attempted to speak, but was only able to produce a guttural choke as he clawed at the foot lodged squarely in his neck.

"As a sanctioned representative of the current democratically elected government, GENEPOL has assessed your continued existence to be a detriment to society and definitive action will be taken," continued Mr. Smith. "In accordance with the stipulated rules of engagement, I hereby inform you've been tried and found guilty, that your civil privileges have been revoked, and as such your right to council rendered irrelevant."

A surge of movement flashed across Mr. Smith's peripheral vision as he turned to see Ryan Polowski's female companion leap forward from her seat, abandoning her high heel shoes and leather purse in her wake as she careened towards the exit of the bus.

"Judgement has already been passed, Mister Polowski, but I'm obligated to offer you a chance to represent yourself before sentencing is carried out," said Mr. Smith, returning his attention towards his target. "Keeping in mind, I'm the only one who can hear you."

"Who, who... are... yo, you?" choked Ryan Polowski.

Mr. Smith paused before speaking.

"I'm the Gene Police," spoke Mr. Smith. "For the good of all mankind."

Mr. Smith leaned forward, placed the barrel of his pistol squarely against Ryan Polowski's forehead, and then flexed his finger against the trigger.

The sound of the gunshot reverberated throughout the interior of the bus as Ryan Polowski's body spasmed and blood cascaded across the window of the bus. Mr. Smith removed his foot from his target's neck, replacing his pistol inside his jacket as Ryan Polowski's listless body collapsed down onto the floor.

Bending over to pick up the lone shell casing, Mr. Smith walked to the front of the vehicle and stepped down through the door of the bus onto the desolate city street. After pausing to examine his surroundings, Mr. Smith sprinted forward into the darkness as the sound of sirens approached in the distance.

Two

"All elements in position, I confirm H-Hour now... execute, execute, execute."

Seated in the command suite of his armoured personnel carrier, John Bishop watched on the situational awareness monitor as the lead elements of his heavily armoured assault team dismounted through the side door of their unmarked transport and advanced towards the indistinct sub-urban home on the opposite side of the street.

"No contacts," sounded the radio speaker. "Stacking right."

"Acknowledged," spoke John, keying the transmitter strapped to his bicep. "Advise when in position."

John received the call out for a substantial drug facility operating out of a domestic urban residence only a few hours prior. The reporting originated through human intelligence, likely a concession from an affiliate drug dealer trying to save himself from prosecution, and POLINT assessed that the cell was preparing to relocate leaving limited time for planning and reconnaissance. This would be his thirty-seventh direct action operation in the last two years, and John assessed that the lack of preparation would have negligible impact on the outcome of the mission.

"Set," cracked the speaker.

"Check the door, snake the room," answered John.

As the team lead for the purely kinetic branch of the civilian police force, John was responsible to coordinate short-duration strikes or small scale offensives within hostile environments to capture, destroy, or recover a specific objective. Normally John's team wouldn't have been required to seize a drug lab, but in this case the dealers had used the proceeds from their narcotics trade to procure a substantial collection of heavy weapons, and there was enough illicit firepower available to warrant his intervention.

"Door's locked," the voice whispered over the radio net. "Two badgers seated to the left, one armed on the right."

"Alright, be advised that still leaves one unaccounted for," responded John, keying the handset as he leaned back in his seat. "Breach and clear, advise when complete."

The inside of the personnel carrier was heavily armored, but despite the robust interior the body of the vehicle was intentionally constructed to appear as a derelict delivery truck. The design of the vehicle afforded a high degree of urban camouflage, and John and the three remaining members of the follow-on team were parked directly across the street from the home. The vast array of digital surveillance equipment combined with the close proximity afforded excellent observation of the target area.

John watched on the view screen as his five-man assault team positioned themselves along the front wall of the home. The last man in the line slung his assault rifle, withdrew a pump action shotgun from the holster on his back, and then advanced past the other four members to align himself with the front door. After a visual cue from the man lined closest to the entrance, the lead man took aim with his shotgun and blasted the front door lock into a cloud of splinters. Forcibly kicking the remnants of the door open with the heel of his boot, the breacher stepped away from the doorway as the adjacent team member pitched a grenade through the opening. After an intense flash pulsed across the video feed, all five members of the heavily armed assault team rapidly filed into the entrance of the home.

John stared at the monitor. Although he couldn't see inside the house and the radio net was silent, John had been in command of the direct action response team long enough to know that there was a time for orders, and there was a time to be quiet and let his team do their job. John didn't have to wait long until he heard three gunshots in rapid succession, signalling that the assault team had either wounded or killed one of the dealers. The sound of the gunfire was followed immediately by a small green light which sailed through the battered doorway to land in the middle of the front lawn of the home.

"Room clear," spoke an abrupt voice over the radio. "Det up."

"Let's go," said John, signalling to the remainder of his team with one hand and reaching over to pick up his assault rifle with the other.

Unlocking the steel access hatch, John and the other three members of the follow-on team dismounted the armored personnel carrier into the street. After securing their ballistic helmets and chambering a round into their assault rifles, the four men advanced towards the building.

"Coming in, main entrance," signalled John over the radio.

Passing the green glow stick lying in front of the house, John and his detachment entered the building to join the remainder of their team.

Surveying the interior of the home, John could make out what appeared to be a kitchen to his right. The room was polluted with garbage, and John couldn't discern if the disarray was a result of the kinetic engagement which had just transpired or the unsanitary people living in the home. Lying on the floor of the kitchen was one of the drug dealers, and while his legs were limp and emanating blood across the tile flooring, he exhibited clear signs of life as he yelled obscenities at the DART member leaning over to secure his hands behind his back.

John turned to his immediate left towards a run-down living room. Two couches were angled towards a very expensive OLED television positioned on top of a plastic crate, with a low rising table covered in bottles, magazines, and miscellaneous drug paraphernalia positioned in the center of the room. Resting face down on the floor with their hands tied tightly behind their backs were two additional dealers, both remaining silent as a member of John's assault team stared down at them through the black face shield of his protective helmet.

John looked over at the far side of the room and saw a third member of the assault team standing off to the side of a staircase with his weapon to his shoulder, patiently staring over the sights of his rifle as he watched up the stairway.

John heard a door close and turned to his right to see the fourth and fifth members of the DART assault element approach, and the lead man lifted his face shield as he began to speak.

"Sir, we just came up from the basement," said Saunders, pointing over to a door in the corner of the room. "There's God's own quantity of drugs and chemicals down there, and this whole building is liable to explode."

"That sounds like a lot," answered John. "I'll call in ordinance disposal after we're done sorting this mess out."

"As for the rest, three badgers down," said Saunders, turning to face the rest of the room. "As you can see, one of them was non-compliant."

"We'll get Redford to patch him up before CIVPOL arrives," responded John. "What's going on over here?"

"There's still one upstairs, and we've got him cordoned off," said Saunders, pointing towards the stairway. "He's armed with one hostage, female, probably his girlfriend or one of their customers, and he's threatened to kill her if we approach."

"Classic," answered John. "I'll see what I can do."

"Are you sure that's a good idea, Sir?" questioned Saunders, raising his eyebrow. "We could hand this over to CIVPOL regulars and just wait him out... he's not going anywhere."

"You're probably right," admitted John. "But I'm here now, and the last thing this guy deserves is an easy way out."

"Well good luck with that, Sir," said Saunders, smiling and exhaling sharply.

"Anything else I should know?" asked John.

Saunders paused, slowly looking around the room.

"Room clear," spoke Saunders, shrugging his shoulders.

"I noticed," responded John as he turned towards the center of the room. "Nice work."

John crossed the living room and halted at the bottom of the staircase. Nodding in acknowledgement at the DART member covering the stairs, John looked up at the dimly lit landing at the top of the second floor.

"Hey!" yelled John, attempting to gain the attention of the final member of the drug cell.

"Screw you, pig!" yelled a voice from the top of the stairs.

"My name is John Bishop," yelled John. "I'm from CIVPOL."

"Screw you pig," yelled the voice, his speech accented with obvious panic.

"You just said that!" yelled John.

John returned a glance from the DART member standing beside him and then shook his head before attempting to communicate with the criminal once more.

"My name is John Bishop, and I'm here representing CIVPOL," repeated John. "I'm here to talk to you."

"Talk?" questioned the voice. "What's there to talk about?"

"I'm assuming that there is something that we can offer you," yelled John.

John stared upwards, but only silence followed from the room upstairs.

"I guess he's new at this," said John.

John removed the sling from around his neck and handed off his rifle to the DART member standing next to him.

"Look, I'm coming up," yelled John, stepping forward onto the first step. "I'm alone and unarmed... do not shoot."

"You try anything funny, pig, and I'm going to start blasting," yelled the voice.

"You have my word," responded John. "I'm here to ensure that the situation ends peacefully."

John advanced cautiously up the staircase until he reached the landing at the top of the stairs.

The second floor of the house was covered in darkness, but John could make out the faint reflection of a bathroom mirror coming from the room to his front, the glow of an antiquated computer system and a make shift office to his right, and he could hear stifled breathing echoing down the corridor to his left. John advanced through the hallway and the sound of the movement intensified as he approached the doorway at the end of the corridor. Reaching inside of the blackened room and running his hand up the edge of the wall, John's fingers brushed over a light switch and he was instantly greeted by the sight of a disgruntled man standing against the far wall of a dishevelled bedroom and gripping a tearful young woman to his chest. The man scowled involuntarily at the light, and then quickly extended his arm over the woman's shoulder to point a slim revolver directly at John.

"Stop right there pig!" screamed the man, sounding as if he was trying to speak all of the words of his threat simultaneously.

"Woah... easy big guy!" said John, raising his outstretched palms in front of his chest. "There's no need to shoot anything that you might regret."

"Stay there, right there, in the doorway," spoke the man, sounding more confident as he gripped the woman closer.

John's eyes locked with the hostage clutched against the man's chest. She had a youthful appearance but her face was tarnished with fear, her frantic breathing slowing as she stared back at John.

"Is this your girlfriend?" asked John. "I'm not an expert with relationships, but I can tell you that this is going to cost you."

"Shut up!" yelled the man, crushing the woman towards him and causing her to scream.

"Alright, but that's the reason that I came up here," retorted John, taking a step back and lifting his hands. "So I'll stop talking and you start... what would it take for you to let that woman go?"

The man became still and stared back at John. After a pensive moment to evaluate the offer, the man breathed heavily and began to speak.

"First, you pigs can start by getting the hell out of here," said the man, waving his revolver over his head. "Then, I want a car, a nice one, parked out front."

John nodded his head passively.

"I want some money as well, fifty thousand in cash," continued the man. "Then once I've gotten everything, I'm leaving."

"Anything else?" asked John, raising an eyebrow.

"Yeah," said the man, pulling his arm inward to place the barrel of the revolver against the woman's head. "I'm taking her with me just in case you pigs try to follow me, and you can have her back once I'm far enough away."

John looked over at the woman and then back at the man holding the gun.

"I'll see what I can do," answered John, reaching down towards his belt.

"Hey!" yelled the man, snapping his arm out to aim the barrel of the gun over at John.

"Woah, easy friend!" responded John, displaying his palms towards the man.

The man gritted his teeth and gripped his hostage around the neck with his forearm.

"You've asked for my men to withdraw, a new car, and a small fortune," said John. "This isn't a game show, and you are not the grand prize winner... I'm going to help you, but I need to make a few phone calls first."

The man held still, and after careful deliberation motioned with his revolver for John to continue.

Holding one hand in front of his body, John reached down to his belt to release the plastic clasp on the tactical pouch attached to his belt. John reached inside the pouch and placed his hand tightly around the flash grenade inside, flipping off the safety clip with his index finger and drawing the pull ring away from the body of the grenade with his thumb. Lifting his arm sharply away from his body, the grenade rose up from John's outstretched palm as he reached up to his helmet with his opposite hand and slammed the protective shield down over his face.

"That's not a cell pho…" spoke the man, but his words were cut off.

The grenade sailed into the center of the room before igniting into a ball of searing light and a deafening blast reverberated through the confines of the compact bedroom. The man holding the revolver released his grip on the woman, his face contorting into a twisted grimace of pain as he reached up with his free hand to cover his eyes. John side stepped and positioned himself against the wall as the man fell forward, his right hand clenching to blindly discharge the firearm into the corridor leading into the room. John paused for both the man and his hostage to collapse onto the floor and then stepped forward to firmly plant his boot down on the man's hand still clenching the revolver.

John reached behind his back to remove a set of thick plastic ties from his belt and began to secure the incapacitated drug dealer, and only a few seconds elapsed before he could hear booted feet rush up the stairs of the home.

"Coming in!" yelled a voice from the corridor.

Two DART members surged into the bedroom with their rifles shouldered and their face shields drawn down. After scanning the room over the barrels of their rifles, the two men lowered their weapons and then positioned themselves on either side of the entrance to the room.

"Woah… nice work, Sir," said Saunders, pulling back his face shield. "That didn't take very long."

After cinching the plastic straps closed to secure the man's hands behind his back, John stood up, kicked the drug dealer's revolver across the floor, and removed a glow stick from his chest rig. John looked over and gave an exhausted smile to Saunders, snapping the glow stick with his thumb.

"We're done here," spoke John, dropping the green glow stick onto the ground as he advanced through the door to the room. "Room clear."

Three

"John Bishop, owner."

After a series of audible mechanical clicks, John turned the handle on the door.

"Welcome home, Mister Bishop," spoke an electronic voice. "You have no new messages."

"Good," spoke John, closing the door behind him as the lights to his apartment illuminated.

John removed his shoes and placed his jacket in his front closet. Taking a pensive breath, John flexed his shoulders and leaned his head to one side.

"Ugh," sighed John. "I'm getting too old for this."

John walked out into his living room and looked out the panel windows overlooking the skyline of the city.

"Television on," spoke John. "Local news broadcast."

"Acknowledged," responded the voice.

John turned towards the wall-mounted television, freezing as the screen illuminated. Momentarily mentally fractured by déjà vu, John instantly recognized the images despite the overdubbed commentary of the news reporter.

"Members of the DART were called in response to a drug production facility established in this quiet sub-urban home," spoke the assertive voice of the female new s reporter. "A representative from CIVPOL reported that a large quantity of narcotics and weapons were seized, one hostage rescued, and all four members of the cartel were seriously wounded in the exchange."

"We only shot one of them, and it's not like he didn't deserve it," said John. "Thirty-seven direct action operations, and the media has yet to get a single story right."

"Please confirm your voice command," spoke the electronic voice.

"Not you, dammit!" grimaced John. "I was talking to the television."

"Your Horizon three thousand series television is not equipped with voice recognition software," answered the voice. "Would you like to download a firmware update?"

"Stop it!" yelled John. "But what you can do is email this video clip for me, distribution list direct action response team alpha."

"Acknowledged," spoke the voice. "Would you like to enable video compression to optimize the file for ease of distribu…"

"Just do it!" yelled John.

"Acknowledged," responded the voice.

"Thank you," said John. "How much beer is left… and yes, I realize what time it is."

"There are currently six times three hundred and forty-one millilitre bottles of Magaline remaining in the refrigerator," spoke the voice.

"That won't last very long," said John. "I'd probably have more if you didn't cause me to drink so heavi…"

John paused.

"I'm sorry, I do not understand your request," spoke the voice, breaking the silence. "Please repeat your command."

"Volume, television," said John. "Now."

"Please specify whether you would like to increase or decrease the current volume of the television and by which increment," replied the female voice.

"Full volume!" yelled John. "One of these days I'm going to find out where you are and smash you into a million pieces you digital b…"

John's voice was cut off as the television erupted to drown the apartment with the inane chatter of the two television news broadcasters.

John moved cautiously from the center of his living room and placed his back against the far wall of his apartment. Instinctively reaching to his belt, John instantly realized that while his sidearm was safely stowed in the CIVPOL weapon's lock up, his pistol was not where he needed at this exact moment. With his back pressed up against the wall, John slowly moved towards the entrance of his bedroom until he was close enough to peer into the blackened room, and rising up to block out the ambient light was the clear silhouette of a man towering across the doorway.

John stepped forward with his left foot, raised his right knee, and then thrust his body weight forward as he rammed his right foot through the bedroom door.

The anguished voice of a man roared from behind the door, the pained yell rising over the sound of a commercial for bathroom cleaning supplies blaring from the television. John placed his right foot behind him to steady himself, and then raised his leg again and repeated the strike with equal cruelty. A similar but less volatile cry emanated from the doorway, followed by an audible crash as the unknown intruder bounced off the bedroom wall and collapsed down onto the floor.

"Television off!" yelled John.

"Acknowledged," boomed the electronic female voice over the noise blasting from the television.

Instantly the apartment fell silent and John held in place, listening for movement but hearing nothing.

"Call the police," spoke John. "This location, authenticate, charlie six eight, three…"

John fell silent as the figure emerged from the bedroom and halted in the doorway. Standing to his front was an enormous man wearing a black suit and sunglasses, towering across the door as he stared down at John through the black lenses of his glasses.

"Acknowledged request for immediate assistance," said the female voice. "Please confirm authentication code."

"Never mind!" yelled John, quickly stepping back and preparing to defend himself.

The bear-like man stepped forward, raising his arms as he lumbered towards John. Realizing that he would need to go on the offensive to avoid being instantly overwhelmed by the brutish invader, John darted forward between the man's arms and shot out his left hand. John's palm struck the man on the chin, and he could feel the man's heavy jaw snap shut as his head jolted backwards. Stepping back from his opponent, John snapped out his left foot to strike his opponent cruelly in the knee and cause the gigantic man to collapse sideways down onto the floor.

"How... the hell... did you... get in here!" spurted John as he flailed the intruder with overhand punches.

"John!" yelled the heavy set man, his voice bellowing up from the floor.

John pulled his right foot back to lash out with a kick, but paused in response to the sound of his name.

"John!" repeated the man.

"How do you know my name?" questioned John, holding his foot back and remaining poised for a subsequent attack.

"John, it's me!" said the man.

"Take your hands away from your face!" demanded John. "I can't understand what you're saying."

"Well stop hitting me then!" answered the large man, a spark of adrenaline accenting his speech.

John exhaled sharply, lowering his foot to take a step back from the mammoth trespasser.

"Who are you, and why are you in my home!" blurted John, his question sounding more like a demand than an inquiry.

"John, it's me," said the man, pulling his arms down around his chest. "It's me… Miller!"

"Miller?" questioned John.

John watched as the man reached up with his bulky hand to pull his sun glasses up around the top of his head.

"Don't you remember me?" said the large man, dropping his hands to his sides.

"Miller?" questioned John, his face glowering over with confusion. "Of course I remember you!"

"Well, I'm glad," said Miller, reaching down to rub his left knee. "It's been a long time, and I wasn't sure if you would recognize me."

John approached the man and bent forward , but then paused.

"Miller, my first inclination was to help you up," said John. "But maybe you should tell me what you're doing here first."

"Well, that's fair enough given the circumstances," responded Miller, lifting his bulky torso up off the floor. "Stand down Hogan… we're good here."

John looked over to where Miller was speaking and a second man in a dark suit, a taller, lankier version of Miller, emerged from John's bedroom to stand beside the doorway. John took a step back and raised his hands, unsure if the possibility of a physical altercation still remained.

"Ugh," grimaced John as he clenched his fists. "Who the hell are you?"

"It's alright, John," said Miller quickly, flashing the palms of his thick hands. "He's with me."

"We were fire team partners in the DART for three years," spoke John, turning back to face Miller and dropping his hands to his sides. "Is this what you've been doing since then, breaking into people's homes?"

"I don't break into... well, I suppose that's not exactly true," said Miller, correcting himself.

"Miller, what are you doing here?" questioned John, an anxious tone growing in his voice. "Most people just knock at the front door, and I'm not even sure how you got in here."

John stared Miller directly in the eyes.

"We're here to help deliver a message," spoke Miller.

"A message?" questioned John, unsure of what he was hearing.

"We weren't trying to kidnap you, hurt you, steal your television, peek at you in the shower, or do anything like that," said Miller. "We're just here to deliver a message."

"Well couldn't you have phoned or sent an email o r something!" yelled John.

"We needed to make sure that you were alone and that the area was secure," answered Miller. "There can't be any record of anything that we do."

"So you decided to break into my house?" questioned John. "I almost killed you!"

"I'll admit, I've done better work," said Miller, staring down at the carpet between his legs. "Saying that you almost killed me might be going too far... you just winded me."

John glared back at Miller. Still confused by the situation but willing to admit that his friend meant him no harm, John leaned over, grabbed Miller's arm, and helped pull the massive man up off the floor.

"So, what's this message?" spoke John, sighing sharply. "I'm going to start punching again if you try to sell me something."

"Actually, we typically don't do the talking," answered Miller, groaning as he stood up straight. "We're just the escorts."

"Escorts?" questioned John. "For who?"

"For me," spoke a voice.

John turned to the sound of the voice to see a domineering but dignified man dressed in a pressed black suit and tie standing in the front entrance of his living room.

"Good God," spoke John. "Is there anyone else hiding in my apartment?"

"Records indicate that you are currently the only one in the apartment unit," spoke the robotic female voice.

"Shut up!" yelled John, raising his head to scream at the ceiling.

"Cease all function, time now," spoke the man in the black suit and tie. "Authenticate senior one."

"Acknowledged," spoke the electronic voice. "Goodbye."

John rolled his eyes up at the ceiling, and after a moment of standing in silence turned to face the inauspicious man who had just materialized in his living room.

"So that's how you got in here," said John. "My promiscuous computer let you in."

"Exactly," spoke the man in the black suit.

The man in the black suit stepped into the center of the room, extending his open palm as he moved forward.

"Hello, Mister Bishop, I'm very pleased to finally meet you," said the man in the black suit, holding out his hand as he spoke. "My name is Mister Smith."

"Mister Smith?" questioned John, looking down at the man in the black suit's hand. "You've got to be kidding me."

"Yes… I get that a lot," responded Mr. Smith, lowering his hand to his side. "The irony is that Smith is my real name, if you choose to believe that."

"You seem to know a lot about me, to include where I live," said John, glancing over at the two men standing to his left. "But I'm guessing that all I'm going to get out of you right now is your favorite color."

"That would be a valid assumption," responded Mr. Smith.

"That's what I thought you'd say," said John. "So why don't we cut any further introductions and skip to the part about why you're in my home."

Mr. Smith stared back at John for a moment before responding.

"I expected nothing less from you, Mister Bishop, and you are correct that there is no need to waste any more time," said Mr. Smith. "My associates and I are here to deliver a message."

"Well," responded John, raising one eyebrow. "What is it?"

"I have a proposal for you, Mister Bishop," spoke Mr. Smith. "Please, come with me."

Four

"I'm afraid to ask, but are we almost there?" asked John. "When I agreed to this sales pitch, I didn't expect it to take all day."

John was seated in the back of a practical but very expensive black sedan. The insides of the windows were coated with a black tint, and combined with a thick metallic panel which separated the driver from the rear of the vehicle, the passengers were deprived of any situational awareness of the surrounding area. While he wasn't handcuffed or restrained, stuck between Miller and a car door with the handle removed gave John the distinct impression that he wasn't free to leave.

"This is just a formality, John," said Miller. "Smith will explain everything when we get there."

"We've been driving in a circle for almost an hour now, I get it already," responded John, growing increasingly irate. "Can you at least tell me where there is?"

Miller looked over and stared at John, and then turned back towards the front of the vehicle.

"Headquarters," said Miller.

"Headquarters," sighed John. "Right."

Realizing that at least for the immediate future his questions would go unanswered, John waited in silence until he felt the vehicle slow and then shifted forward to descend downward. Finally, the vehicle turned once more before stopping abruptly.

"We're here," said Miller.

Miller leaned forward in his seat and banged on the blacked out passenger window and both doors of the sedan immediately opened. John exited the vehicle to find himself in a well-lit underground parking garage. The parkade was similar to every other parking garage that John had ever been inside, with the exception that each row of parking stalls was filled by the identical black sedan.

"Wow, this is super-secret," said John. "I'm glad you escorted me all the way out here to see this."

"Our headquarters has five levels, Mister Bishop," answered Mr. Smith, closing the passenger door of the vehicle behind him. "This… this is just the parking lot."

Mr. Smith motioned for John to follow and advanced down the center of the garage.

"Don't forget where we parked," said John, slamming the car door closed and stepping forward to fall in behind Mr. Smith and the other two escorts.

The four men crossed to the far side of the parking lot until they reached an access elevator with a large steel door, and John watched as Miller reached up with his ponderous hand to press a singular red call button. Instantly the doors to the elevator divided, and John followed Mr. Smith and his entourage inside.

"If you've been keeping track, this is the underground parking garage," said Mr. Smith as the door to the elevator sealed shut. "This is the only entrance to the building."

"Let me guess what's next," smiled John, looking down to survey Mr. Smith's suit and tie. "Your tailor?"

"No," said Mr. Smith as the doors to the access elevators opened. "Security... please remain very close to me at all times."

Following Mr. Smith out of the elevator, John was met by the sight of four heavily armoured guards armed with assault rifles. The security guards bore a stark resemblance to the members of his direct action team, but their mat colored body armor was sanitized of any form of rank, insignia, or identifying markers. Two guards stood on either side of a lone security door built into an imposing reinforced steel wall rising up to the ceiling. A thick metal shutter hung immediately over the doorway, and John could make out at least an additional four security guards standing on the opposite side of the door.

John watched as one of the guards stepped forward, silently handing off a small card to Mr. Smith before returning to his position beside the door.

"Here," said Mr. Smith, turning to John and extending his hand. "Put this on."

John looked down to see that Mr. Smith was holding a plastic white security clip badge. John took the card, and after turning the security badge over in his hand to find that the other side of the card was also devoid of any markings, John sighed and clipped the badge to the front pocket of his shirt.

"Make sure that you don't take that off, and that it's visible and all times," said Mr. Smith. "Otherwise things might get unnecessarily... messy."

"Fair enough," said John, as he surveyed the stoic heavily armed guards occupying the room. "You can never have too much security."

"Follow me," said Mr. Smith.

John paused as Mr. Smith advanced towards the security door, and as he passed through the steel entrance a female electronic voice resonated throughout the room.

"Smith, agent," spoke the voice. "Armed, access unlimited."

From the other side of the doorway, Mr. Smith turned and motioned for John to advance. John nodded his head, and then cautiously stepped through the doorway.

"Guest, unassigned," spoke the voice. "Unarmed, escort required."

"I thought security at the airport was bad," said John, turning to watch Miller and the second escort pass through the door. "But now that I'm inside, can you tell me what I'm doing here?"

"Patience, Mister Bishop," said Mr. Smith, turning towards the far side of the room. "We're almost there."

John followed Mr. Smith as they crossed the floor and the remaining security guards parted to reveal the reflective doors of an elevator. When they reached the far wall, Mr. Smith reached up and held his thumb against a panel embedded into the wall adjacent to the elevator doors. The panel instantly lit up to display a digital keypad, and John watched as Mr. Smith entered a numeric code. After the sixteenth digit, John looked down at the floor and shook his head.

"You know, that's a real fire hazard," said John.

"You said it yourself, Mister Bishop," said Mr. Smith, as he keyed the final entry and the doors to the elevator slid open. "You can never have too much security."

Mr. Smith stepped forward into the elevator, and John moved to follow but felt a heavy hand grasp his left shoulder. John quickly turned in response to the contentious gesture to see Miller smiling back down at him.

"This is where we part ways, good buddy," said Miller, lowering his arm and taking a step back. "My job ended when we passed through that door."

"The only door," responded John, motioning towards the imposing security door. "I suppose that makes your job that much easier."

Miller smiled, and then extended his arm to shake John's hand.

"I hope you take Smith up on his offer," said Miller, squeezing John's hand. "We could use someone like you."

"Right, but I'm not even sure where here is yet," said John. "All I know so far is that you guys seem big on matching outfits."

"Smith will explain everything, and you're being asked to fill a… a more select position than what I do," responded Miller, releasing John's hand. "Just remember that the right thing to do isn't always the most human."

John stared blankly back at Miller, unsure of how to respond.

"Those are big words for a guy like you, Miller," said John, smiling at his friend's sudden change in disposition. "I think that's the first intellectual thing that I've ever heard you say."

"Well, I like to leave the thinking to people like you and Smith," said Miller. "For me, I just do what I'm told and soldier on, just like what we've always done, and the only difference is here the uniforms are much, much cooler."

"Thanks Miller," responded John. "If a guy like you works here, how bad could it be?"

"Good luck, John, and remember what I said," spoke Miller, his smile dissipating.

John nodded his head in acknowledgement, and then turned to join Mr. Smith as the elevator doors closed behind him.

"So I have been keeping track," said John, looking around the featureless interior of the elevator. "I'm taking it that we're headed to the second floor."

"That is correct, Mister Bishop," answered Mr. Smith, staring ahead at the elevator doors. "We're headed to the operations centre."

"Operations centre?" asked John, turning to look over at Mr. Smith. "The operations centre for what?"

"The Gene Police, Mister Bishop," spoke Mr. Smith as the doors to the elevator divided opened. "Welcome to the headquarters for the Gene Police."

Five

"I'm sorry, the what?" asked John, following Mr. Smith out of the elevator. "Did you just say… oh my God."

"I don't believe in God, Mister Bishop," replied Mr. Smith, turning to address John. "But if God did exist, he would work here."

Overcome by his surroundings, John stammered forward onto the second floor of the building.

John was standing at the base of an expansive tiered room. Six sequentially larger circular echelons extended towards the ceiling, with two opposing stairways running up either side of the enclosure to connect a concrete walkway encircling each level. Each tier was lined with a myriad of computer terminals, monitors, and surveillance equipment, with an operator positioned behind each station. A steel circular table with a computer monitor embedded into the surface rose up from the center of the room, and three men stood around the table stoically watching the display.

"This, as I've already mentioned, is our operations centre," spoke Mr. Smith, raising his arm to highlight the room behind him. "Although if you do decide to take up our offer, you won't be spending much time here."

"There must be fifty people working in here," said John, angling his head back to examine the upper levels of the room.

"Fifty two to be exact, including the commander," responded Mr. Smith, pointing to the display in the center of the room. "We control everything from here to include personal tracking, surveillance, intelligence reporting, essential logistics… all in support of our operations."

John ceased his inspection of the room and looked over at Mr. Smith.

"The Gene Police?" questioned John.

"The Gene Police is just a colloquialism," answered Mr. Smith. "Our official title is GENEPOL, although you won't find us in the phone book."

"And what does GENEPOL do exactly?" questioned John, raising one eyebrow. "I'm not a scientist, so I'm not sure why you brought me here."

Mr. Smith paused to stare at John, seemingly gauging the best way to deliver his response.

"Have you ever heard the acronym BLUF before, Mister Bishop?" asked Mr. Smith.

"Bottom line up front," responded John. "Basically code for don't waste my time."

"Exactly," answered Mr. Smith. "The bottom line for GENEPOL is we kill off the bottom one thousandth percent of the population annually."

John froze, unable to mentally discern what he was hearing.

"I'm sorry," blurted John, leaning towards Mr. Smith. "What did you just say?"

"You asked me what GENEPOL does, Mister Bishop, and I'm telling you," answered Mr. Smith. "The purpose of GENEPOL is to exterminate a small percentage of the population each year, specifically the bottom one thousandth percent."

John glared back at Mr. Smith, and then lowered his eyes to stare down at the floor.

"Allow me to try and explain," spoke Mr. Smith, breaking the silence.

"Yes, I think... I think you should," said John, passively nodding his head.

"The motivation behind GENEPOL's inception is that we live in an age of complete security, Mister Bishop," said Mr. Smith, placing the palm of his hand over his opposing fist. "Everyone, absolutely everyone, has access to a socialist collective network free of war, conflict, disease, and hunger, which guarantees the universal preservation of individual rights and freedoms."

"That doesn't sound so bad," said John, looking back up at Mr. Smith. "That's the main reason why I became a police officer."

"We live in a society where everyone is safe, secure, and free of any kind of threat or competition," continued Mr. Smith. "But what I've just described isn't the whole truth, is it?"

"Then what is the truth?" asked John, hesitant of what the response might be.

"The reality is that as a result of the pursuit of a utopian society, we've virtually eliminated the concept of evolution," answered Mr. Smith. "Through the insistent preservation of boundless freedoms, humanity has lost all direction, stagnated, and begun to collapse in on itself."

"So that's your solution to all of society's problems?" questioned John, stepping towards Mr. Smith. "To start killing people?"

"Look around in the streets, Mister Bishop, and what do you see?" asked Mr. Smith. "Criminals, thieves, street gangs, drug dealers and addicts, pickpocket accountants,

49

corrupt bureaucrats, the lethargic, the ignorant, and the perverse… you of all people should appreciate that reality."

"What do you mean by that?" asked John, recoiling at the personal nature of Mr. Smith's narrative.

"You're a police officer, Mister Bishop, a member of the DART no less," said Mr. Smith. "All you deal with is the scum of humanity, the people that the civilian police force isn't even willing to deal with."

"Yes, but I don't kill them!" answered John, throwing his hands in the air.

"Well, why not?" questioned Mr. Smith.

"I'm no philosophy major, but I'd say because it's unethical… and not to mention illegal," spoke John, surprised by the conviction of his own response.

"Is that it?" asked Mr. Smith.

"Is what it?" questioned John.

"Morality and legality," responded Mr. Smith. "In your mind and by your personal standards, are those the only two factors restraining us from rightfully ending the lives of the people who would best serve society dead rather than alive?"

"I hadn't given it much thought," answered John sharply. "But those are the two points that immediately come to mind."

"Fair enough, but allow me to address your point regarding the ethics of our operation by asking you a question," said Mr. Smith, pressing his finger-tips together. "What, by your definition, is morality?"

"Well if I remember correctly, it's the difference between right and wrong," answered John sarcastically. "That's what we have a legal system for."

"We have a legal system where we temporarily sentence criminals to jail, but then we let them go to freely procreate and spawn more drug dealers, thugs, and miscreants, and those are just the ones that we catch," spoke Mr. Smith. "It's a cycle that will repeat and expand over and over until there is nothing left but human garbage... all for the sake of saying to ourselves that we haven't done anything wrong."

John glared back at Mr. Smith, still attempting to comprehend the magnitude of what he was hearing.

"Did you know that there is an inverse relationship between intelligence and birth rate, Mister Bishop?" asked Mr. Smith.

"To be honest, I've never thought about it," answered John.

"Basically humanity is becoming slower, weaker, and increasingly self-indulgent with each passing generation," said Mr. Smith. "It's up to us to cull the herd."

"Being dumb doesn't necessarily make you a criminal," interjected John.

"Not necessarily," answered Mr. Smith. "But I don't recall the last time that I saw a research scientist hold up a liquor store."

John paused, lifting his eyebrow back at Mr. Smith.

"That was a joke, Mister Bishop, but I use it to make a point," continued Mr. Smith. "If you're focused on the ethics of killing one person, you're thinking too small on too short a time frame, and in the same moral terms which placed humanity in this mess in the first place."

"Well, how should I be thinking?" asked John, looking up at the room around him. "How would you justify all this?"

"Think big, Mister Bishop," answered Mr. Smith. "The goal of the Gene Police is to stop civilization's downward spiral and free ourselves from the detriment of human malignancy."

John exhaled sharply, taking a step back and running his hand over his forehead.

"I'm taking it that you're still not convinced," spoke Mr. Smith, stepping forward. "You mentioned the legality of our operation, and as a police officer, perhaps you'd like me to explain."

"You can try," responded John. "The last time I checked, no judicial system in the world would allow anything like this."

"I assure you, Mister Bishop, nothing we do here is illegal," said Mr. Smith.

"Are you sure?" questioned John.

"GENEPOL was initiated and legislated by the government to combat a perpetually increasing crime rate and to contend with the innate imperfections of the rule of law," spoke Mr. Smith. "Our actions and our stipulated rules of engagement are completely sanctioned, albeit covertly, by the government."

"Which government?" asked John.

"All of them," responded Mr. Smith. "Key leadership at the federal, state, and municipal levels… although that's the extent of who knows about our existence."

John's mind flashed to the last federal election, shuddering at the unintentionally lethal implications of his vote.

"Isn't... isn't someone going to, you know, eventually figure all of this out?" asked John, feeling a surge of nausea swelling in his stomach.

"Figure what out?" responded Mr. Smith. "The fact that one in every thousand people living in this city disappears or meets an unscheduled demise each year?"

"Yes, exactly," slurred John, feeling as if he had just walked into a trap.

"Well, Mister Bishop, two things," said Mr. Smith, looking up at the towering array of operators and computer consoles filling the room. "First, GENEPOL is more established then you might think, and we've been doing this for some time now."

"How long?" asked John.

Mr. Smith's head snapped back towards John, glaring him directly in the eyes.

"You're not the first person I've recruited, Mister Bishop," spoke Mr. Smith. "Like I say, we've been doing this for some time, and we've become very... effective, at what we do."

"And no one notices?" interjected John.

"That brings me to my second point, Mister Bishop," answered Mr. Smith. "Arguably the key to why we've been able to operate for so long without interference is GENEPOL's strict adherence to secrecy, security, and anonymity."

"Yes, I've noticed how you like to operate," said John, looking back at the elevator.

"It's for good reason, Mister Bishop, because kill one drug dealer, one thief, one low-life, and no one cares, and in reality the average person would likely celebrate the demise of a worthless criminal," continued Mr. Smith. "However, if the population as a whole ever learned that they were being culled like livestock, the result would be instant chaos."

"You'd be out of a job," said John.

"The human race has become intoxicated by unrelenting personal freedoms," spoke Mr. Smith. "The public can never learn what we do, and our operation must remain a secret."

John starred back at Mr. Smith, feeling physically exhausted from the reality which had suddenly engulfed him.

"Still not convinced?" asked Mr. Smith.

"Would you be surprised if I said that this is a lot to take in?" replied John, reaching up to rub his eyes with his hands.

"No, not at all," answered Mr. Smith. "Do you like power slideshow presentations, Mister Bishop?"

"I absolutely hate them," answered John sharply. "I try to avoid meetings as well as my computer just to get away from them."

"So do I," said Mr. Smith. "I'll let you view the standard presentation that we show to all potential recruits, and deliberately it's only three slides long."

John watched Mr. Smith step towards a flat screen terminal mounted into the adjacent wall and pressed a single button, and the computer terminal came to life to display a simple yet professionally designed line chart.

"Not to insult your intelligence, Mister Bishop, but time runs along the X axis, recorded events running up the Y axis, and each of the lines represents a type of crime or relevant social indicator," spoke Mr. Smith, running his finger along the monitor as he explained the diagram. "These are the statistics taken over the last year, and as you can see for yourself, there is a downward trend in each case."

John cautiously stepped towards the monitor, and as he examined the diagram the uneasy sensation in his stomach intensified.

"Are you all right, Mister Bishop?" asked Mr. Smith.

"Yes, I'm fine," spoke John. "It's just, I didn't expect…"

"For there to be solid empirical justification for the utilitarian nature of the Gene Police?" interrupted Mr. Smith.

"Yes, I suppose that's what I was going to say," responded John, realizing from his prepared response that he was not the first person to have this conversation with Mr. Smith. "How do I know these numbers are accurate, or you haven't changed them to say what you want?"

"Good question," answered Mr. Smith. "Simply these aren't our statistics, they're yours."

"What do you mean by my statistics?" asked John.

"Most of these figures come from the police department, and the remainder from the municipal government," responded Mr. Smith. "GENEPOL doesn't invest any money or man power in producing these reports, but we habitually refer to them as our primary measure of effectiveness."

John looked at the operations floor, and then back over at the screen.

"So you use these graphs to justify what you do here?" asked John.

"Numbers don't lie, Mister Bishop," spoke Mr. Smith, pointing back at the screen. "The total number of incarcerated inmates is down five percent over the last year, armed robbery down three percent, tax evasion down two percent, drug trafficking down five percent, and the number of homeless is down a massive twelve percent."

"Is that because you kill a lot of homeless people?" interjected John.

"It's because we kill a lot of homeless people, Mister Bishop," snapped Mr. Smith. "Also these figures are just what were recorded over the last year."

Mr. Smith reached out and tapped the monitor. In response to his touch, the line graph changed to a second, similar chart.

"This is the same reporting, but these figures represent the impact over time since the inception of GENEPOL," spoke Mr. Smith, tracing the lines on the graph with his finger. "As you can see, there is a substantial downward trend."

Mr. Smith reached up and tapped the monitor a second time, and the screen flashed to a third diagram.

"Finally, this diagram extrapolates GENEPOL's impact over the course of the next fifty to one hundred years," said Mr. Smith. "If it wasn't self-evident, you can see GENEPOL's relevance over humanity's future."

John followed the lines on the graph with his eyes. Each line arced gradually downward and bottomed out along the zero mark over time.

"That concludes this portion of the briefing," said Mr. Smith, reaching over to power off the monitor. "Do you have any questions at this time, Mister Bishop?"

"I'd never thought that a power slideshow presentation would actually make me sick," responded John, looking down at the floor.

"Most of our potential recruits have a similar reaction," said Mr. Smith. "If you choose to join us, we're placing a substantial amount of responsibility in your hands."

"If I choose," answered John.

Mr. Smith shot his eyes back at John as he quickly stepped forward to press the call button beside the elevator door.

"If you're still undecided, then let's move onto something more interesting, Mister Bishop," said Mr. Smith, stepping into the elevator as the doors parted open.

"What exactly do you mean by interesting?" asked John, slowly following Mr. Smith into the elevator. "I'm not sure how much more of this I can handle."

"Interesting, as in what's in all of this for you," answered Mr. Smith, as the elevator doors sealed shut behind them.

Six

"There are five floors in GENEPOL headquarters, not including the motor pool," spoke Mr. Smith. "You've seen security and the operations centre, and now I'm going to show you the remainder of our headquarters."

"You said you were going to show me something more interesting," said John, looking up at the electronic floor indicator lights running along the top of the elevator door.

"Patience, Mister Bishop," responded Mr. Smith. "There are few who have seen what you've seen or learned what you now know, and our time together is almost complete."

The doors of the elevator jarred open to reveal an expansive floor illuminated by fluorescent lights cutting across to the far side of the ceiling. On the left hand side of the floor John could see rows of lockers lined along the wall encircling an assembly of workbenches and tables stacked with various pieces of electronics and equipment. Looking to his right, John could make out a series of reinforced glass rooms, with each section containing targetry, weapons, training mats, and hanging heavy punching bags.

"This is our training and load out centre," spoke Mr. Smith, reaching his hand out to hold the elevator door. "Any weapons, supplies, or equipment that you need is located on this floor… anything you can imagine, we have."

"That is interesting," said John, his eyes widening as he looked out over the vast array of weapons, devices, and tactical paraphernalia dispersed across the room. "I can imagine quite a lot."

"One of the major advantages of working for us is that we will be able to equip you with everything that CIVPOL was either unable or unwilling to provide," responded Mr. Smith, turning towards John. "Make no mistake, we do have a budget, but it's a lot larger and with a lot less red tape attached than you're probably used to."

"Will I get a black suit like yours?" smiled John.

"Several," answered Mr. Smith, removing his hand from the door and allowing the elevator to close.

Mr. Smith reached down and pressed the call button for the next floor and the elevator jarred upwards. John watched as the floor indicator light flashed one position to the right and the doors parted open.

"This, this is the A and A floor," sighed Mr. Smith. "Accommodations and administration."

John leaned forward to peer out of the elevator. Similar to the previous floor, the entire storey was divided by a row of lights which ran to the other side of the building. The left side of the floor resembled a generic hotel with numbered doors running down the length of the hallway, and the opposite side of the room appeared as a stereotypical office building with desks, filing cabinets, and computer terminals spread throughout a maze of cubical walls.

"Ugh," grimaced John, pulling himself back inside the elevator. "This is... less interesting."

"Nobody cares about accommodations and administration," said Mr. Smith. "This is where you can perform personal background checks or rest if you need to, with the only point to note being that you'll have to cook your own food."

"Why's that?" asked John.

"We try to maintain the number of employees to the absolute minimum for operational security reasons, so we don't hire cooks or support staff," responded Mr. Smith. "The end state being that you need to look after yourself."

"Makes sense," said John.

"Now let's head to the final floor," spoke Mr. Smith, pressing the top call button on the elevator control panel.

"Hopefully it will be more motivating than the A and A floor," said John as the elevator door closed.

"I assure you that the top floor is the most unique part of our headquarters, Mister Bishop, and with the possible exception of the operations centre, also the most vital ," spoke Mr. Smith.

John looked over at Mr. Smith as the elevator shifted upward. Given all that he had seen already, John was unsure if he should be concerned, captivated, or afraid of what was to follow. John waited silently as the floor indicator jumped to the far right hand position and the polished elevator doors divided open.

"Follow me, Mister Bishop," spoke Mr. Smith as he stepped onto the final floor of the GENEPOL tower.

John stepped out of the elevator into an immense open room several times the size as any of the previous floors. The expansive enclosure was cool and dimly lit, but John could make out four identical rows of computer server towers running across the room to intersect the base of a colossal electronic tower extending upwards towards the ceiling. The room was silent with the exception of a low resonating hum emitting from the expansive array of computer equipment all operating in unison.

"My God," spoke John, reeling forward at the sight of the floor.

"This is what we like to refer to at GENEPOL as the Cypher," spoke Mr. Smith, turning to address John.

"It's massive," said John. "Can you play solitaire on that thing?"

"I'm sure you could, Mister Bishop," replied Mr. Smith. "But as one of the most powerful computer systems in existence, we tend to use the Cypher's application for much more productive purposes."

"Such as?" asked John. "To find out who hasn't been paying their taxes?"

"That's part of it, Mister Bishop," responded Mr. Smith. "Please, follow me."

Mr. Smith motioned for John to follow, stepping forward to walk between the two center rows of computer servers towards the tower at the far side of the room.

"The Cypher is just a computer system, albeit a very powerful one, and like any computer we use it to calculate a series of algorithms," spoke Mr. Smith as he advanced forward. "There is nothing remarkable about the process in itself, however the algorithms themselves are quite unique."

"What do you mean?" asked John. "What's so special about your... your algorithms?"

"GENEPOL starts by inputting every single person in the city into the computer, we constantly update their status, and ideally track their exact whereabouts," responded Mr.

Smith. "Then we run each entry against a series of specific predetermined moral, social, and economic criteria in order to rank their collective worth, or hindrance, as the case may be."

"I, I don't understand," stuttered John.

"It's simple, Mister Bishop, every action an individual makes moves them up or down the list," spoke Mr. Smith. "A misdemeanor moves you down the list, a felony way down, making a donation or charitable work moves you up, poor financial history, down, voting, up, working more than forty hours a week, up, a prolonged criminal history, down, owning your own property, up, not owning a home, down, not having any home, way down, education, up, no education, down, and not paying your taxes… well, I'd highly recommend that you don't forget to pay yours."

Mr. Smith stopped at the base of the computer tower, raising his head to look up at the Cypher.

"The end product of our algorithms is a list of every single person in the city, all ranked according to their social merit," continued Mr. Smith. "Is this all starting to make sense to you now, Mister Bishop?"

"This is like a bed time story that you tell your kids to scare them into behaving themselves," responded John, reaching out to gently touch the oppressive computer system.

"Yes, but there's a difference between us and a ghost story," said Mr. Smith. "The Gene Police are real."

"So, what happens next?" asked John, genuinely apprehensive of what the response might be.

"What happens next, Mister Bishop, is simple mathematics," answered Mr. Smith. "How many people live in this city?"

"Roughly five million," said John.

"Exactly five million, two hundred and fifty six thousand, nine hundred and eighty two as of this morning, but for the purposes of our discussion, close enough," said Mr. Smith. "And five million divided by one thousand is... Mister Bishop?"

John looked over at Mr. Smith, a sinking sensation of horrible realization coming over him.

"Five thousand," spoke John. "You kill five thousand people, every year."

"Five thousand deserving individuals, Mister Bishop," said Mr. Smith. "Five thousand, divided by twelve months, divided by thirty GENEPOL operatives, gives you this."

Mr. Smith turned towards a solitary control panel embedded into the base of the towering computer, pressed two buttons on a numeric keypad, and then placed his thumb against an adjacent biometric reader. Instantly a low buzzing sound emanated from the immense machine, and a single grey sheet of paper ejected from a thin metal slot set into the center of the tower. John watched as Mr. Smith reached out and tore off the printout, turning towards him and then holding out the piece of paper.

John cautiously reached out to take the grey sheet from Mr. Smith. Turning the paper over, John examined the page.

"Fourteen," spoke John. "Fourteen names."

"Thirteen point eight to be exact," responded Mr. Smith. "But here at the Gene Police, we round up."

"So basically, after all that you've shown me, you're asking me to kill the fourteen people listed on this page," said John as he stared down at the sheet of paper.

"There are currently twenty-nine GENEPOL operators working within this city, and if you decide to join us, that will make a total of thirty," responded Mr. Smith. "Given current population levels, fourteen, no more, no less, is the number of targets that each operator is required to prosecute each month."

"Every month," whispered John to himself.

"As I mentioned, Mister Bishop, we've been doing this for some time now," spoke Mr. Smith. "I completely understand the implications of what I'm asking you to do."

John said nothing as he studied the page in his hand, running his finger down the list of names on the electronic printout.

"We've come to the end of my briefing, Mister Bishop, and the end of GENEPOL's proposal," spoke Mr. Smith, breaking the silence. "Do you have any questions or require any further information from me before you make your decision?"

John looked up at Mr. Smith.

"I have two questions," answered John.

"Go ahead, Mister Bishop," asked Mr. Smith. "The time for questions is now."

"First, you're asking me to commit unadulterated atrocities and give up my job, my life, and essentially my humanity," said John. "How much am I going to get paid for giving up everything I have?"

"Good question, Mister Bishop," responded Mr. Smith. "If you're still not convinced, and being a practical man, you will appreciate the fact that you will be incredibly well paid."

"How well?" prompted John.

"Each newly recruited GENEPOL operator starts by earning a quarter of a million per year, increasing by four percent per annum," answered Mr. Smith.

"That is a lot to consider," said John, raising his eyebrows.

"GENEPOL has a substantial budget, but the money is only a means to finance an effective operation by hiring, but also retaining, the best people available," said Mister Bishop. "We also provide a robust pension as an incentive for our retirees to quietly disappear."

"Okay, one final question," spoke John, gauging the best way to phrase his inquiry. "What happens exactly if I say no?"

"To date, no one has ever said no, Mister Bishop, but the answer is quite simple," responded Mr. Smith. "Absolutely nothing."

"Nothing?" questioned John. "Nothing at all?"

"If you say no, Mister Bishop, you turn around now, go back down the elevator, and my associates will escort you back to your home, your job, and your life," said Mr. Smith. "This is your opportunity to take, which means it is also yours to turn away."

"It's that simple, is it?" asked John, looking across the room at the elevator door.

"Yes, it is, Mister Bishop, but with the caveat that join us or not, if you mention one word about our operation to anyone, no matter how subtle, we will know," spoke Mr. Smith. "Then you will disappear like the thousands of other malignant individuals who've helped the world by ceasing to exist."

"I see," said John, looking back down at the list of names on the page.

"Any further questions, Mister Bishop?" asked Mr. Smith.

"No," said John. "No further questions."

John looked back over at the elevator door, then up at the computer system ascending beside him, and then back at Mr. Smith.

"Do you remember the drug cell that the DART intercepted?" asked Mr. Smith, sensing John's hesitation.

"Of course I remember, I haven't even had a chance... wait a minute," interjected John, cinching his eyes back at Mr. Smith. "What has that got to do with this?"

"When we approached you, Mister Bishop, you were watching the news report on television," continued Mr.

Smith. "Without going into too much detail, I can tell you that waiting for subsequent coverage of the trial would be a complete waste of time."

John glared back at Mr. Smith, silently preparing himself for any further concluding revelations.

"You've actually been working for us for some time now, Mister Bishop, you just didn't know it," said Mr. Smith. "It seems only appropriate for you to formally join our ranks."

Mr. Smith stepped forward, extending his arm towards John.

"Do you accept?" questioned Mr. Smith, holding his hand out in front of John. "This will be your one and only opportunity, Mister Bishop."

For a lucid moment, John recalled why he became a police officer, and how all he ever wanted to do was use his strength to help others. For the first time in his life, John was being offered the opportunity to protect more than just the people in immediate need, but to safeguard society as a whole by pre-empting the evil that existed in this world.

John extended his arm and gripped Mr. Smith's hand, realizing that he had either just made the best decision or the worst mistake of his entire life.

"Welcome to the Gene Police, Mister Bishop," spoke Mr. Smith.

"Thank you," said John, unsure of what to say.

"We're fortunate to have an operator with your level of expertise and experience," said Mr. Smith.

Mr. Smith released John's hand, nodded quickly, and then turned to head towards the elevator.

"Wait!" snapped John. "What the hell am I supposed to do now?"

"Simple, Mister Bishop," responded Mr. Smith, speaking over his shoulder as he marched towards the far side of the room. "Go home."

"What?" blurted John. "Go home, and do what?"

"Everything you need to do your job is being delivered to your apartment as we speak," answered Mr. Smith.

"What…oh no, not again," said John to himself, remember how he'd found Miller and another unnamed thug inside of his home once already.

"You'll find seven issue black suits, a bank card linked to your pay account, an equipment case, a cellular phone, and a new sidearm," continued Mr. Smith. "You'll also find a single copy of the GENEPOL handbook."

"Handbook?" asked John. "The Gene Police has a handbook?"

"The handbook is the only formal training that you'll received, Mister Bishop, in addition to everything that I've just told you," spoke Mr. Smith, halting momentarily to glare back at John. "As clandestine as it is for security reasons, I highly recommend that you read the handbook in its entirety."

"Okay," said John. "But I'm still not sure..."

"I wouldn't have recruited you if I didn't think you'd be able to figure it out, Mister Bishop, but since you're new, you may want to start off easy," interrupted Mr. Smith as he planted his palm onto the elevator call button. "I'd recommend starting from the bottom of the list, and working your way up."

"The bottom?" asked John. "Why's that?"

"Because the people at the bottom of the list tend to be stupider and easier to kill," yelled Mr. Smith as he stepped through the elevator doors.

"Oh yeah," said John, glancing up at the Cypher. "That actually kind of makes sense."

"For the good of all mankind, Mister Bishop, and good luck," said Mr. Smith, his voice echoing from the confines of the metallic elevator walls.

"Right," said John to himself, looking down at the list of names in his hand. "For the good of all mankind."

"Remember what I said, Mister Bishop," yelled Mr. Smith as the elevator doors sealed closed. "And don't forget to read the handbook!"

Seven

John looked down at his watch. It was time to begin.

Following Mr. Smith's advice, John decided to start with the last of the fourteen names on his target manifest. John's target, his very first target as a GENEPOL operative, was a man named Jack Lawson.

After a hasty but heavily questioned resignation from his responsibilities as the direct action team lead, John quickly shifted his attention towards gathering as much background information on Mr. Lawson as possible. Using the impressive intelligence gathering resources at GENEPOL headquarters, John learned that Jack Lawson was a lifetime professional felon whose criminal resume included smuggling, drug trafficking and distribution, the sale of stolen vehicles, and money laundering. John also discovered that Mr. Smith hadn't exaggerated the self-destructive implications of neglecting to pay taxes. Jack Lawson had failed to file his tax return for the current fiscal year, and combining his extensive criminal history with a marked deficit of social contributions, Mr. Lawson had unknowingly flagged himself for immediate termination.

John took an entire week to survey Jack Lawson, track and confirm his movements, and then finally formulate a plan to prosecute his first target. John's initial plan was to pose as a potential client looking to purchase black market firearms, arrange to meet Mr. Lawson in a secluded location, and then swiftly execute him during the transaction. John eventually decided against this idea as it was highly unlikely that Jack Lawson would attend an illicit arms deal by himself, and other members of his distribution team including dedicated armed security would almost certainly be present. John needed to isolate his target, and while Lawson's associates were probably not the most upstanding citizens either, he was only mandated to kill Jack Lawson, minimize any collateral damage, and draw as little attention to himself and GENEPOL as possible.

After spending a week mentally designing and subsequently rejecting plan after plan on how to proceed, John finally admitted that he wasn't a police officer anymore. Recognizing the need to quickly reverse deep-seated indoctrination stemming from years of service as a peacekeeper, John delineated a course of action that was cold, unsophisticated, and without even a semblance of honor.

John would simply follow Jack Lawson back to his home, break into his house in the middle of the night, and then discretely execute his target in his sleep.

Looking up from his watch, John stared out at the lifeless sub-urban home. The house appeared vacant, but despite the lack of activity no one had entered or exited the premises since he had followed Lawson home from work a few hours prior. John pressed open the car door and stepped out from his vehicle, glancing up and down the darkened street as he gently closed the door behind him. Sensing the still of the night air and confident that he would be able to execute his plan without witness or interruption, John turned to cross to the opposite side of the street.

This being his first official break and enter, John was apprehensive about how to reliably proceed. From his experience, the irony about criminals is that they tend to take their personal security even more seriously than the average law abiding citizen. Assuming that there could be high security locks, motion detectors, and trip alarms on all of the entrances, John decided to follow the path of least resistance and simply gain entry through the front door.

John advanced down a stone pathway dividing the front lawn of the home and then slowly crept up a short set of concrete stairs leading to the main entrance. Through the glow of the ambient street light, John could make out a standard lock and a heavy deadbolt securing the door. While his actions c ouldn't be considered entirely ethical, nothing that John had done up until this point in time was definitively illegal. Reaching into his back pocket to draw his lock picks, John mentally prepared himself to formally cross over from a devout protector of the law to a self-assumed sociopathic killer.

John froze in place as a discernable clicking noise emitted from the lock followed by an immediate rush of air as the door swung open. Mentally dislocated on how to react, John remained motionless with his hand stuck in his back pocket as a stocky man wearing a poorly tailored grey suit stepped out into the doorway.

"Hey man, I thought I heard someone," spoke the short man, arching his head back to address John. "Where have you been?"

"Yeah," slurred John. "I got lost."

"How could you get lost?" asked the man. "Don't you deliver for a living?"

Hesitant of what to say, John squinted his eyes together and looked out at the street behind him.

"It's dark out," spoke John, turning back towards the man. "I couldn't find the place."

The stocky man grinned fervently back at John, seemingly deriving meaning from his last gesture.

"I hear that!" blurted the short man as he laughed up at the doorframe. "I once drove in circles around my own block and didn't stop until my car ran out of gas… that was the highest that I've ever been!"

John smiled and nodded his head, attempting to feign insight into the man's humor.

"Come on in, man," said the short man, smiling as he pulled the door open. "Nice suit by the way."

"Thanks," responded John, retracting his hand from his back pocket and following the short man inside the home.

John stepped through the front door into a blackened living room. Everything was dark except for a low blue haze emanating from an adjacent room, and from what John could make out the house was well furnished and extensively complimented by the profits from Lawson's illicit business.

"Follow me, man," said the short man, closing and locking the door behind him.

"Mind if I leave my shoes on?" asked John. "I've got other deliveries to make tonight and I won't be able to stay."

"Oh, no worries, man," responded the short man. "It's not my house!"

The man laughed to himself as he crossed the living room floor to disappear into the adjoining room. Questioning whether or not he was about to make a colossal mistake, John followed the short man and approached the cloud of blue light.

John stepped through the doorway and quickly surveyed the room. Everything was dark with the exception of a blanket of blue light which swelled up from the base of the walls as the subdued tone of an esoteric electronica track cyclically pulsed from the surrounding stereo system. In the center of the room was a leather couch with three men slouched over a low rising wooden coffee table. Recliners were positioned on opposite sides of the room with a tall slovenly man occupying the chair to John's left and the stocky man which he had previously encounter seated to the right. Standing in the doorway to an adjacent room was a woman dressed in tight dark clothing, leaning her head against the doorframe as she stared passively in at the remainder of the group.

John's arrival seemed to rouse the occupants of the room, and the collection of men simultaneously stirred and straightened in their seats as he approached the gathering.

"Where the hell have you been," demanded the man sitting in the middle seat of the couch. "You were supposed to be here three hours ago."

"He got lost!" said the short man, tossing his head back in the recliner and laughing uncontrollably.

The man in the middle of the couch leaned forward in his seat, looked John directly in the eyes, and then gradually smiled.

"You're new," spoke the man. "What's your name?"

"Adrienne," answered John, instantly regretting not being able to come up with a more masculine pseudonym.

"Alright, well you're here now," continued the man. "If the delay is an indication of how good this stuff is, it will have been worth the wait."

"You're Lawson?" asked John softly.

"Yeah, that's me," answered the man.

"Good," said John. "I just wanted to make sure."

"Well you're in the right place, and it's time to get this party back on track," responded Lawson, relaxing back into his chair. "You got my stuff?"

"Yeah," answered John. "I've got what you're looking for right here."

As the room watched in anticipation, John reached inside his jacket with his left hand. In one fluid motion, John removed his taser pistol from the holster, extended his arm towards the man seated on the left hand side of the couch, and then pulled the trigger. The device discharged and two electrodes jettisoned forward to strike the man in the throat, his limbs instantly curling towards his chest as he collapsed down onto the floor.

Responding to John's attack, the room erupted. A collective series of shouts rose up from the floor as Lawson spastically pushed himself upwards to dive behind the couch, the woman in to doorway turned to run but stumbled forward into the adjacent wall, and the remaining men scrambled to get to their feet.

John reached down with his free hand to draw a baton from his belt, and clenching his fist as the metal rod extend, John arced his arm overhead and slammed the end of the baton down onto the tall man struggling to come to his feet. The lofty man crumpled headfirst into the coffee table as John side stepped to the right and kicked out with his leg to strike the short man attempting to flee the room. John's foot struck the stocky man in the back, and due to the significant weight differential between the two men, the short man careened forward through the adjacent doorway and forcefully vanished from the room. The remaining man seated on the right side of the couch bounded forward, crashing over the remnants of the coffee table as he hooked his outstretched fist towards John's head. John ducked underneath the attack by dropping to his knees, and angling his left arm upwards, John discharged the secondary round from his taser into the advancing man's groin. The man jerked his head towards the ceiling to release a hollow shriek as John stood up and rammed the tip of his baton into the man's chest, retracting the telescopic rod and knocking the man callously back down into the couch.

"Okay," spoke John, simultaneously replacing his baton to his belt and his stun gun to his holster. "That went as well as it could have, I suppose."

John advanced forward, stepping over the incapacitated men and broken furniture strewn across the floor. Finding nothing on the opposite side of the couch, John looked over to see the woman staring back at him from the corner of the room.

"Please!" shrieked the woman, exhaling in sobbing gasps. "Don't hurt me!"

"On one condition," spoke John. "Where is he, Lawson, where did he go?"

"There," cried the woman, lifting her hand off the floor and extending her finger.

John looked in the direction the woman was indicating to see a corridor set into the far wall. John surged into the hallway, sprinting past multiple darkened rooms until he reached a partially open door outlined by the city lights radiating from outside. John slammed the door open with his shoulder and leapt down a short set of stairs into an unkempt backyard filled with newspaper, cans, and miscellaneous garbage bordered by a low rising wooden fence. A narrow alley ran along the far side of the yard, and a flicker of movement raced across John's peripheral vision along the alleyway to his left. Rushing forward and smashing open the wooden gate leading into the yard with his foot, John sprinted down the alley towards the shadow in the distance.

John continued for only a few seconds before he reached his target. As he closed in, John could see Lawson staggering through the dark, gasping for air as he stumbled down the alleyway. John surged forward, crossing his arms across his chest before ramming into Lawson from behind. John planted his foot to halt his momentum as Lawson lurched forward, colliding with the ground and skidding facedown along the gravel alley. John quickly stepped forward, crushing Lawson's hand underneath his left foot and then placing his opposite knee at base of his downed quarry's neck.

"I'm going to let you in a little secret about druggies, Lawson," spoke John, reaching over to grab Lawson's free hand and pin his arm behind his back. "They always try to run, despite the fact that they're all in terrible shape."

"What do you want from me, man!" screamed Lawson as he attempted to press himself off the ground. "I've got money, and it's yours if you let me go!"

"I don't want your money, Jack," responded John, twisting Lawson's arm to preclude any further resistance.

"Well... what do you want from me then!" yelled Lawson.

"Jack Lawson, you've been tried and found guilty under article zero zero one of the GENEPOL charter," spoke John slowly, stumbling to remember the GENEPOL Miranda rights. "As a responsible representative of, um, the government, and in accordance with the rules of engagement, I hereby inform you that... that you are guilty, that your civil privileges have been revoked, and um... that you will no longer need your phone call."

"What the hell is that supposed to mean!" spurted Lawson, straining his neck to look up at John.

"It means... it means I need you to stop living," said John. "Do you have anything to say for yourself?"

"What!" screamed Lawson, bucking violently and attempting to struggle free of John's hold. "I didn't do anything!"

"Criminals always think that they're not the bad guy, Lawson," replied John, sighing and relaxing his grip. "I'm starting to think that they actually believe themselves."

John quickly looked down the alleyway and then reached into his suit jacket with his free hand to withdraw a long silver pen. Flicking off the pocket clip with his thumb, John held his hand up to see the ambient street light reflect across a short surgical needle extending out from the tip of the pen.

"They said... they said that this wouldn't hurt," spoke John, carefully turning the pen over in his hand.

John raised his hand above his head, pressed his thumb firmly on to the top of the pen, and then stabbed the needle down into the back of Lawson's neck.

"Stop!" screamed Lawson as he spasmed against the ground.

John released his grip and fell backwards, passively kneeling down as Lawson rolled out from underneath him. John examined the spent injector in his hand before closing his eyes and taking in an absorbing deep breath. Remaining still, John could hear Jack Lawson dragging his feet along the gravel in an attempt to flee, and only a few moments elapsed before the panicked footsteps dissipated and the distinct sound of a body colliding with the ground swept across the alleyway.

Eight

"That was crude, unprofessional, disorganized, and you're lucky that you didn't kill someone you weren't supposed to, including yourself."

John honestly didn't care about the crude and unprofessional portion of the commentary as the incident with Jack Lawson may have gotten a little ridiculous, but that didn't change the fact that he had killed his target. However, what did concern John was what Mr. Smith had to say next.

"Your primary concern now should be time. Admittedly Lawson was your very first assignment, but he took a week to dispatch. With thirteen names left on your list, that leaves you with approximately two days to prosecute each of your remaining targets. You will need to work quickly to remain on schedule… for the good of all mankind, out."

Mr. Smith had never explicitly discussed the consequences of failing to reach the required target quota, but then he didn't have to. A pink slip from GENEPOL was more than likely accompanied by an immediate bullet to the face, and if John wanted to keep his own name from appearing on next month's target manifest, he would have to work quickly.

After listening to Mr. Smith's message, John immediately reached into his suit jacket and unfolded his target list. Studying the remaining names on the page, John began to plan.

The second name from the bottom on John's list was a man named Ronald Teaford. Mr. Teaford was the only person on John's target manifest without an associated primary address. After a cursory search of Mr. Teaford's banking records, John quickly realized that attempting to secure Ronald Teaford's home address would be a complete waste of time. The bank repossessed Mr. Teaford's house five years ago, and Ronald Teaford was homeless. This was the reason why John's target manifest did not cite an address, more than likely why GENEPOL wanted Mr. Teaford prosecuted, and also the same reason why John would have to get creative in order to locate his target.

John spent the majority of the next day visiting a series of homeless shelters, finding that a lot of information, albeit often inarticulate, was readily available in exchange for a minute amount of money. When John finally tracked down Ronald Teaford, he was huddled in a dark, very secluded alleyway in an obscure part of the industrial sector. Mr. Teaford had constructed a small shanty house out of old sleeping bags and boxes, and while he initially protested at the intrusion, John was able to subdue his suspicions with a package of cigarettes and some matches. Under the guise that he was a reporter writing an article on the city's homeless population, John spoke to the man long enough to put him at ease and divulge his name. John gave the dishevelled man a chance to laugh about his situation and finish his cigarette, and then pulled out his pistol and shot Ronald Teaford once in the forehead.

The third name on John's target was a young, lower income factory worker living in a dilapidated urban slum named Billy Ray Burnshaw. Despite his modest standard of living, a revoked driver's licence, and a list of other minor infractions, Billy Ray had attracted the Cypher's attention with several convictions of battery and a growing number of reports of domestic violence.

As long as he could remember, John had despised bullies. During his time with CIVPOL, John always held a propensity for violence against anyone who liked to pick on someone either unwilling or unable to defend themselves. While the most difficult aspect of his new employment was the ethical dilemma derived from euthanizing derelict and criminal elements of the population, John was willing to admit that a small part of him was going to take satisfaction in ending Billy Ray Burnshaw's life.

As John began to delineate Billy Ray's demise in his head, he realized that the most important planning factor wasn't Mr. Burnshaw himself, but his wife and family. If John simply walked up and shot Billy Ray, a documented history of domestic violence would lead CIVPOL to his battered wife as the primary suspect. At the very least, indiscriminately killing Billy would leave a family consisting of a stay at home wife with two small children without a source of income. After checking Mr. Burnshaw's financial records, John learned that Billy Ray's manufacturing job featured a substantial life insurance policy blanketed across all employees of the company. If he was somewhat Machiavellian in orchestrating Mr. Burnshaw's death to look like an accident, John would not only rid the world of a bully, but also create a lucrative future for Billy Ray Burnshaw's wife and children.

Despite his good intentions, John's thought process immediately fractured. Fashioning a murder to look like an accident was an act that criminals had been attempting to perfect since the inception of the rule of law, and while the concept wasn't new, John was undecided about how to begin. Searching for homicidal inspiration, John ran an open source search on the leading causes of accidental death, and according to the municipal department of statistics and record keeping, the number one cause of preventable fatalities was motor vehicle accidents.

"I wish I had more time to be creative," said John as he rammed his foot down onto the accelerator of his vehicle.

Exiting his home and stepping off the curb to cross the street to the nearby bus stop, Billy Ray Burnshaw only had a moment to turn his head before the front grill of the speeding black sedan dominated his field of vision. The front bumper of the vehicle impacted Billy Ray just below the knee cap causing his body to slam into the hood and slide up onto the windshield. John stomped on the brakes, bringing the vehicle to an immediate stop and jettisoning Billy Ray's bullish physique forward. Pausing to watch his target land motionlessly in the middle of the street, John gently lifted his foot off the brake pedal and waited until the vehicle jolted upwards once along the front axle and then again along the rear before speeding away.

Unlike the previous three, John prosecuted his fourth target by accident.

The episode with Billy Ray Burnshaw left a relatively noticeable impression in the front of his car, and after returning to GENEPOL headquarters to exchange his vehicle, John headed home to rest. On the freeway leading to his apartment, John watched a grey luxury sedan speed past him on the inside lane, hastily swerving and cutting in and out of traffic. Surmising that the vehicle was more than likely driven by someone of a criminal nature as opposed to a pregnant woman ready to give birth, John accelerated and pursued the speeding vehicle along the expressway.

Relaying the license plate through GENEPOL, John learned that the driver of the vehicle was a man named Conrad Morganstern. Mr. Morganstern record's indicated he was a relatively accomplished lawyer and maintained his own practice as a legal tax consultant. However, John also confirmed that Conrad Morganstern possessed three prior convictions of driving under the influence, and despite his legal history, Mr. Morganstern had obviously not learned his lesson. Unfortunately for Conrad, his dangerous driving habits had attracted the attention of a member of the Gene Police with a schedule to keep.

Processing a hasty rules of engagement request through central, John followed the erratic vehicle onto the freeway off-ramp and down through a series of side streets leading into an upper-middle class residential portion of the city. John pulled over to the side of the road and watched as his newly acquired target pulled into a driveway, knocking over a line of garbage cans stacked along the sidewalk before coming to a stop.

John opened his car door and approached the luxury sedan from the rear and watched as the driver stumbled backwards out of his vehicle and then turned to kick the car door closed behind him. Realizing that he had just locked his keys inside of his car, the man finally stood up and slammed his fists down on the top of the vehicle.

"Do you need some help?" asked John.

Finally noticing that he wasn't alone, the man turned to focus on the stranger standing in his driveway.

"Are you from the motor vehicle association?" slurred the man, hanging onto his car for balance. "Man... that was really fast!"

"Not exactly," responded John. "Are you Conrad Morganstern?"

"I think so," replied the man as his body gently swayed back and forth. "This is his house, those are his keys locked in the car, and this is the lawn where he is going to sleep tonight."

After pausing to survey his target's slouched and disorganized posture, John quickly admitted that there was no reason to embellish or derive an overly contrived solution as to why he was here. John reached into his jacket, drew out his pistol, and shot Conrad Morganstern once in the chest.

John only found out later that killing a target under an approved rules of engagement request counted against his monthly GENEPOL quota. While he didn't take complete satisfaction in gunning Conrad Morganstern down on the front lawn of his home, his demise meant that John only needed to prosecute thirteen targets instead of fourteen.

Unfolding his target manifest, John could feel his confidence growing as he examined the next name on his list.

John's fifth target was a computer programmer named Joseph Wong. Joseph was just one man, and from a solely corporeal perspective he occupied a small physical footprint living in a tiny apartment located in a downtrodden part of the city. However, from a virtual point of view, Joseph Wong's signature was louder than a New Year's Eve firework celebration observable from space. Joe Wong was the single largest online spammer currently operating in the city and responsible for hundreds of thousands of unsolicited digital messages advertising defective products or fraudulent investments each year. Joseph was extremely adept at his chosen career, but just like all the other individuals who had worked their way onto the Cypher's list, his actions were a substantial moral and fiscal drain on social infrastructure while offering nothing in return.

Given his flamboyant digital presence, GENEPOL easily identified the originating internet protocol and confirmed Joseph Wong's home address. After checking his personal records to verify that he lived alone, John didn't waste time with an intricate plan and simply knocked on the front door of Joseph's apartment. As soon as he heard an audible click emanate from the door handle, John raised his knee to his chest and pummeled the front door open with his foot. John stepped through the doorway to find Joseph Wong curled up on the floor clutching his bleeding face, and after spurting off the GENEPOL Miranda Rights, John shot Joseph Wong once in the head. Admitting that every computer owner in the world would appreciate the gesture, John hastily ripped the network of computers lining the apartment out from the wall before exiting through the window and descending to the street below.

John's next target was a man named George Mooney, or at least that was one of his names. George Mooney went by many handles such as George Munson, George Landal, George Nelson, but George Louis Mooney was his real name. George was a professional debtor, and he made a living out of spending other people's money. About once every year, George would establish an intricately crafted alternate identity and proceed to draw money, lines of credit, and as much financial backing from as many banking institutions as possible before collapsing his false persona and disappearing back behind the anonymity of his real identity. In addition, devoid of any formal source of income and remaining officially unemployed for his entire adult life, George had yet to make a single tax contribution. After finally correlating the digital signature block of each of his pseudonyms to his real identity, GENEPOL identified George Mooney as a fiscal parasite and scheduled him for immediate prosecution.

Completing a review of his financial records, John learned that George Mooney unsurprisingly still lived with his parents. To avoid another debacle similar to the incident with Jack Lawson, John needed to draw George away from his home, his family, and any prospective witnesses. Given George Mooney's vice for fraudulent credit abuse, John devised the answer almost instantly.

John made a request through the chief financial operator at GENEPOL to produce a phoney credit card and associated authentication letter, addressing the card to Mr. Mooney's latest alternate identity, George Richard Martin. On activation, John would receive the exact location of any purchases or withdrawals made with the new card. After dropping the letter into George's mailbox, John waited only a few hours until he received a call from central and raced to a convenience store located near George Mooney's home.

John pulled into the parking lot of the store and immediately spotted a slovenly man wearing a crumpled t-shirt and torn sweat pants through the front window of the store. John waited until the man ceased his fervent attempts to withdraw money from the automated teller machine and exited the store into the parking lot. John followed the man while uttering the GENEPOL Miranda rights before stopping his car and rolling down the window.

"Hey, George," yelled John, attempting to signal the man without sounding overly pervasive.

As the corpulent man ceased his journey across the parking lot and turned towards the sound of his name, John withdrew his pistol and held his arm out the car window, took careful aim at George's head as he rotated towards him, and then pulled the trigger.

The subsequent and seventh name of John's list was a woman by the name of Susan Day.

Nine

The first meeting that John was asked to attend, although calling it a meeting may have been inaccurate as Mr. Smith was the only one speaking, was the first time that John had ever seen any of the other operators. Dressed in identical black business suits, all thirty operatives arrayed themselves along the circular interior of the GENEPOL operations centre, staring up in unison as Mr. Smith addressed his audience.

"All morality, or at least perceived morality, stems from humanity's will to survive and procreate, and some would even claim that life is a right as opposed to a responsibility," spoke Mr. Smith, raising his arms to point up at the situational awareness monitors lining the interior of the room. "As you all know, there are groups of individuals, be it convicts, degenerates, miscreants, the weak and the evil, that need to be denied their professed right to exist in order to benefit the greater social order."

Mr. Smith continued, lowering his gaze to stare out at the unbroken line of silhouettes surrounding him.

"That is the purpose of the Gene Police, to remove the collective detriments to society and allow humanity to progress, evolve, and to thrive," said Mr. Smith. "Our ultimate goal is not to protect ourselves in the present, but to secure a meaningful future for everyone... for the good of all mankind."

At the time, everything that Mr. Smith had said seemed to make sense. Mr. Smith's cold logic imbued John with an irrefutable sense of purpose, a responsibility not only to the public, but a trans-generational obligation to the entire human race. However, as John stared up at Susan Day's decaying apartment building, realizing what he was about to do, Mr. Smith's motivational speech seemed to be of little consolation.

John may have been old fashioned, but there was something about killing a woman that definitely did not appeal to him.

John advanced up the concrete stairs leading to Susan Day's apartment complex and approached the front door. After easily defeating the dated locking system, John conducted a final visual sweep of the street behind him and then stepped through the front entrance to the building.

GENEPOL never explicitly disclosed why they wanted an individual killed off, but John quickly realized that they didn't need to. With each of John's previous targets, there was a distinct instance when the justification as to why each name appeared on his list became exceedingly clear. For John's current target, that moment was when he stepped inside Susan Day's apartment complex.

Appraising his surroundings as he passed through the front hall, John assessed that he didn't need to be an accountant to know that this building would be cheaper to demolish than attempt to restore, and presumably the only incentive to actually live here was incredibly low monthly rent payments. Chipped paint and antiquated carpet lined the interior of the apartment with sections of torn wallpaper pulled back to reveal the worn brick structure, and despite the wind drafting through a broken window on the far side of the hallway, an obvious negligence towards sanitation contaminated the air. Removing his target list from his pocket to confirm Susan Day's apartment number one final time, John progressed up the stairwell as the sound of his footsteps creaked throughout the building.

From his background checks, John learned that Susan Day was essentially a social derelict. She was unemployed, uneducated, with no known public or private affiliations of any kind. From her financial records, Ms. Day apparently only left the house to purchase pharmaceuticals, and her net worth was in constant decline. From what John could gather, Susan Day wasn't a bad person and her criminal record was free of any documented convictions, but if her dilapidated living accommodations were indicative of the rest of her life, there was no ambiguity as to why the Gene Police wanted her dead.

Cresting the stairs to the top floor, John turned down a narrow corridor passing the sounds of unruly disputes, animated laughter, and inane television banter exuding from each doorway until he reached the last apartment on the left. John turned his head to simultaneously watch back down the hallway while placing his ear against the door. Other than the low tremor of an ancient boiler system permeating up through the walls, John was unable to detect any signs of movement and reached down for the door knob. As the handle turned in his hand, John concluded that Susan Day must be either very trusting, lazy, forgetful, or a combination of all three. Regardless of the reason, Ms. Day's apathy towards her personal security was working to his advantage, and as objectionable as his task may be, John admitted that his present target was rapidly becoming the most effortless to prosecute. Turning the handle until he heard a faint click, John carefully pressed open the door and crept through the opening.

John quickly surveyed the interior of the residence as he gently shut the door behind him. The apartment was dark with the exception of small shards of light piercing through the windows and highlighting the outline of the room. Through the obscurity, John could make out a small kitchen to his left, a living area to his front, and two doors set into the wall to his right. The entire living space was barren with vacant counter tops, unadorned walls, with the few pieces of remaining furniture scattered out across the living room floor.

The apartment appeared to have been abandoned, and John began to question the accuracy of GENEPOL's records as he crept forward. John carefully glanced through the doors to his right to find a bathroom and a bedroom, both unoccupied and mirroring the desolation of the remainder of the home. Stepping towards the window set into the far wall of the living room, John looked out at the street outside and sighed. As he was met by the faint scent of cigarette smoke, John froze in place.

"Are you here from the bank?" questioned a pale voice from behind him.

Keeping his hands at his sides and instinctively refraining from making any contentious movements, John turned away from the window towards the sound of the voice.

"I walked right passed you," stuttered John. "I mean... I didn't think anyone was home."

John took a step forward and his eyes focused on the outline of a woman seated in a wooden chair pressed into the corner of the room. Despite the intrusion the woman remained slouched in her seat, her dark hair running down across her thin face as she stared over at a cigarette clasped in her left hand.

"Susan Day?" asked John.

"You've snuck into the right apartment," answered the woman. "Are you from the bank?"

"Uh, yes Miss Day, I'm from the bank," responded John, quietly hoping that Susan Day didn't think to ask which specific institution he claimed to represent.

"Well, you're a bit late," said Susan, pointing out over her vacant living room. "This is all that's left."

"I'm not here to take your furniture," answered John, looking down at the unbalanced wooden chair Susan Day was seated in.

"Then, why are you in my apartment?" asked Susan.

John paused, instantly recognizing that he wasn't here to interrogate or find out anything more about his target. While GENEPOL obviously possessed enough justification to terminate Susan Day or she wouldn't have been manifested for prosecution, that didn't mean that John didn't hold his own reservations. If John could uncover a reason to clearly substantiate to himself why Susan Day would be better off dead, then a conversation with this woman would be more than worthwhile. All John needed was one despicable fact, one loathsome character trait, to generate a sufficient amount of contempt and suppress his conscious long enough to pull the trigger.

"I'm putting together a report for the bank, Miss Day" said John. "Can I ask you about your financial situation?"

"Go ahead," answer Susan. "I can tell you that it will be a very short report."

"I'm concerned... I mean the bank is concerned about your financial situation," said John, surveying the decrepit apartment.

"I appreciate as much as I'm surprised by your sentiments," responded Susan. "But I'm here for a reason."

"What reason?" asked John.

"It's a fairly simple chain of events," continued Susan. "I have no money because I can't work."

"We're you fired or something?" asked John.

"It's because of my condition," answered Susan. "All the time, money, and energy that I have left goes towards my treatments."

"Treatment?" questioned John. "I don't mean to pry open your life, but I would like to understand the situation."

"The therapy is provided and the only cost is a bus ticket, but it's the medication that takes everything that's left," replied Susan, shaking her head. "The irony being that the treatment I need to stay alive has also killed my back account."

"Cancer treatment?" asked John, grimacing to himself.

"The doctors say that the therapy will help with the pain and the pills with keep me going," said Susan. "At least for a while longer."

"Well if that's true, Miss Day, what about your hair?" asked John, raising one eyebrow.

"Oh, I can't have radiation treatment," said Susan, her voice showing a spark of intonation. "That's the last thing that I want to do."

"Why not?" asked John. "Don't you want to recover?"

"Because it will harm my baby," answered Susan, tugging her shirt up to reveal a noticeably distended abdomen.

John stood up straight, the causality between Susan Day's social dislocation, her desperate financial history, and her austere apartment all finally beginning to connect.

"You're pregnant," said John, realizing that his statement was redundant as soon as he spoke.

"Yes, of course," smiled Susan. "They certainly pick the observant ones to work at the bank."

"Well, we try," said John, unable to think of a more incisive response.

"It's not that I don't want to recover, it's that I don't want to harm my perfect, little one," continued Susan, gently placing her right hand on her stomach. "She's all I have left, and all that's keeping me going."

"So basically... basically you're sacrificing yourself," said John, thinking out loud. "Not accepting radiation treatment so that..."

"I'm not going to make it, but I just need to survive a little while longer," interrupted Susan, staring back at John. "No matter what happens, the bank can't repossess my baby, can they."

"I see," said John. "How much longer?"

"Five weeks, five days," replied Susan Day, tapping her fingers across her stomach. "I just need to hold on till then, and that's all that matters."

John turned his head to look out the window, admitting that his attempts to rationalize killing his target had completely backfired. Susan Day wasn't a criminal, and she wasn't a drug dealer, a vagrant, a bully, an alcoholic, a digital scoundrel, or a serial fraudster. Ms. Day definitely wasn't part of the social elite, but John couldn't help empathizing with her situation and respect her selfless temperament.

John felt sincerely grateful that he had chosen to speak with her, but his sense of appreciation was instantly replaced by complete mental prostration about what to do next.

"May I use your bathroom, Miss Day?" asked John, looking around the darkened apartment.

"Yes, of course," answered Susan Day. "It's one of the few things that actually still works around here."

"Thank you," responded John, nodding his head.

John turned and walked towards the doorway in the far corner of the apartment. Triggering the light switch to reveal a confined bathroom devoid of any personal amenities, John gently closed the door behind him and walked over to the antiquated sink.

"What are you going to do, John?" spoke John, turning on the cold and hot taps simultaneously. "What are you going to do?"

Gripping the edges of the ceramic basin, John raised his head up to the bathroom mirror.

"I don't know yet, but I'll tell you exactly what you're not going to do," said John, turning to look over at the bathroom door. "What you're not going to do is go back into that room and gun down a pregnant woman with cancer... that's exactly what you're not going to do."

John reached out and rubbed his hands together under the water streaming down from the tap.

"But that's why you're here," spoke John, staring down at his hands. "You're here because her name is on the list."

Cupping his hands together under the faucet, John leaned forward to coarsely splash his face with water, scraping his hands down his face before dropping his arms to his sides. Standing up to his reflection, John's mind flashed to the handshake with Mr. Smith, to the faces of all the people he'd killed, and to the present and future lives resting on the other side of the door.

"What have you done, John?" said John, glaring back at himself. "You've made a horrible, horrible mistake."

Exhaling a punctuated breath, John reached forward to shut off the faucet taps, quickly dried his hands and face with the remaining towel, and then turned to open the bathroom door.

"Is everything all right?" asked Susan, leaning forward in her seat.

"Yes," said John, stepping into the centre of the living room. "Everything is completely fine."

"You're sure that you're not here to take more of my furniture?" questioned Susan.

"No, Miss Day," answered John. "I don't want your furniture."

"Well that's good, because I wasn't looking forward to sitting of the floor," smiled Susan. "Is there anything else that you need for your report?"

"Report?" asked John.

"Yes," said Susan. "Your report for the bank."

"Oh, yes, the report," answered John, realizing that he had stumbled over his own lie. "No, everything is very clear to me now."

"Good," said Susan. "I'm glad to know that the bank has our best and brightest looking after our money... or what's left of it in my case."

"Indeed," replied John, taking a step forward. "There is one more thing."

"Yes," asked Susan, a tone of apprehension accenting her voice.

"You shouldn't smoke," answered John. "It's a very bad habit."

"You're absolutely right," sighed Susan, tapping out her cigarette into the arm of her chair. "My little one is all that matters now."

"You're a very brave woman, Miss Day," spoke John, turning to leave. "Thank you for your time."

"If I had something better to do other than wait, I might have been upset," smiled Susan, watching John as he headed for the door. "Can I expect a visit from the bank in the future?"

"No," replied John, speaking over his shoulder as he tore open the front door. "I promise that no one from the bank will ever bother you again."

Ten

"Bishop, agent," spoke the female electronic voice. "Armed, access unlimited."

Stepping through the security door and passing the assembly of armed guards, John advanced towards the elevator on the far side of the GENEPOL security floor. Holding up his thumb to the panel on the wall and inputting the elongated numeric security password, John progressed through the elevator doors and pressed the call button for the top floor. Cognisant of the reality that he might not leave GENEPOL headquarters alive, John turned to look out over the security floor as the entrance to the building disappeared behind the reflective elevator doors.

The elevator began to ascend and John looked up at the floor indicator lights and watched as the far left hand light pulse one position to the right.

John had made a terrible mistake. By agreeing to Mr. Smith's offer, John had willing collaborated with an idealistic delusion of a utopia free of crime and social frailty, and by failing to see the intrinsically malevolent nature of the Gene Police, a lot of people were dead.

John's consolation, the only way that he could rationalize his actions, is that by agreeing to Mr. Smith's offer he had created an opportunity. John was now one of the Gene

Police, and not only did he possess intimate knowledge of the organization, but he was also in the unique position to halt GENEPOL's machinations from within. To protect innocent people like Susan Day, to correct his mistakes and atone for the lives he'd taken, one incontestable thought burned in John's mind.

John stared at the elevator floor indicator as the light flashed to the center position.

John had committed to what he needed to do as soon as he stepped outside of Susan Day's apartment, but while his purpose was clear, his thought process immediately reached an impasse. The question that resounded in John's head was how he was going to single-handedly defeat one of the most insidious organizations in existence.

John quickly admitted to himself that while he was highly trained and experienced, he was unlikely to pick a fight with the other twenty-nine GENEPOL operators, individuals who were just as motivated, capable, and lethal as he was, and have even a remote chance of success. GENEPOL's excessive level of security would also prove incredibly problematic. There was only one entrance to the headquarters protected by eight heavily armed security guards, and other than the encrypted internal operator network, there was no means of communicating from inside the building. Regardless of which plan he committed to,

John would be completely isolated as soon as he entered the building.

Plagued with indecision about how to contend with such an insurmountable opponent, the thought of simply leaving crept into John's mind. John could leave the city, maybe even the country, and try to disappear to a remote part of the world and hope that the Gene Police didn't come looking for him. John finally conceded that if he simply left then nothing would change, and then no one would be able to save people like Susan Day from being killed. GENEPOL would probably find him anyway, and by leaving he would be condemning himself to live the rest of his short life running in fear.

John watched blankly as the elevator floor indicator jumped to the second position from the right.

The plan that John finally decided on was so simple that it almost terrified him.

GENEPOL's entire operation was dependent on a strict adherence to secrecy as the keystone to their survival. Mr. Smith had said himself that if the population ever learned that their civil rights were being covertly violated, then the results would be catastrophic for GENEPOL. If John could take away their anonymity, reveal the existence of the Gene Police, then he would be able to destroy GENEPOL's operation forever.

There was one primary problem with John's plan. John could try telling the entire world about the Gene Police, but there was no reason for anyone, less the most devout conspiracy theorists, to believe anything that he had to say. John needed proof, solid substantiated evidence of the existence of the Gene Police. Fortunately for John, he'd been carrying part of the solution in his jacket pocket ever since his initial meeting with Mr. Smith.

The floor indicator light flashed to the far right hand position and the elevator doors parted open. Taking in an immersive breath, John centered himself and stepped out of the elevator. Advancing between the rows of computer server towers, John headed towards the Cypher at the far side of the room.

John needed the list, one combined target list comprised of thirty target manifests for a total of four hundred and twenty names. John already possessed one GENEPOL target list, however, disseminating his own list wouldn't prove anything other than to clearly identify himself as a certified psychopathic killer. If John could acquire the current target list in its entirety, then he would have sufficient evidence to prove GENEPOL's existence to the public. While t here would be many who would undoubtedly question the meaning or validity of the document, John was confident that even the most devout skeptic would realize the significance once the individuals on the list started to unexpectedly die off if they weren't dead already.

John halted in front of the Cypher, arching his head upwards to look up at the towering machine.

Over the past month, John had learned an extensive amount about the Gene Police including how they were structured, the background behind their exacting ideology, and how they employed their vast array of advanced technology. Out of everything that John had discovered about GENEPOL, the inner workings of the Cypher had proved to be the most disturbing but also the most useful.

The Cypher was the driving source behind GENEPOL's operations. A surreal intelligence network integrating a flood of data from all available sources, the Cypher perpetually recorded the background, location, affiliations, and specific behaviors of every single person in the city. Drawing from an extensive database of personal history, the Cypher subsequently assigned an arbitrary value to the sum on an individual's actions to rank perceived social worth relative to the remainder of the population. Despite the surge of raw information required to accurately compute GENEPOL's social algorithms, the Cypher was only capable of generating one product. As a simple but effective additional security measure designed to further guard GENEPOL's existence, the Cypher's only information output was a one page hard copy target list tailored for each individual GENEPOL operator.

If John wanted the list, he would need to go to the top floor of GENEPOL headquarters, compile the complete target list, and then quickly escape before anyone discovered what he intended to do.

John stepped towards the Cypher, positioning himself in front of the numeric keypad embedded into the center of the tower. Entering the digits zero one into the keypad and then pressing his thumb against the adjacent biometric reader, John watched as a single sheet of grey paper ejected from a thin slot at the base of the gigantic machine.

John reached out and tore off the printout and held the page up to the light. Similar to his own target list, printed on the page in dated dot matrix font was fourteen names listed alongside an associated address. Shuddering at the thought that the majority of the people listed on the page were either dead or actively being hunted, John transferred the piece of paper gently into his left hand and returned his attention to the numeric keypad.

John typed in the number zero two, pressing his thumb against the biometric reader as a second sheet of paper shot out from the body of the massive computer. Repeating this process, John systematically ascended through the corresponding code for each GENEPOL operator until he was holding an orderly stack of thirty sheets of paper.

John knelt down and placed the pages on the ground beside his feet. Reaching into his jacket pocket, John removed a thin rectangular digital scanner and flicked his wrist to extend the device. John placed the scanner on the bottom edge of the paper as a low green light emitted from the digital optical reader and then carefully guided the device to the top of the page. Reaching with his free hand to peel away the page, John returned to the bottom of the stack of paper and slowly swept the scanner over the second page.

Working methodically while trying to avoid driving himself into a panicked state of urgency, only a few minutes elapsed before John reached the final page.

Collapsing the portable scanner between his fingers, John carefully extracted the small memory chip from the side of the scanner before returning the device to his pocket. John reached into his jacket to withdraw his cellular smart phone and then delicately inserted the data chip into the side of the phone. The screen immediately powered on to display an electronic folder containing a single entry, and John selected the file with his thumb as the screen flashed to a digital rendering of the grey sheets of paper. Using his finger to scroll through the document and ensure that the pages had scanned correctly, John exhaled a confident sigh of relief as he counted thirty legible pages.

John closed the document and opened his email browser to the top draft message. Selecting the file attachment icon and then locating the digitized target list, John paused as the document digitally affixed itself to the message and then moved his thumb over the email send icon.

"For the good of all mankind," spoke John, pressing his thumb firmly down onto the send button on his phone.

In response to John's touch, an error message which read "no signal" flashed in predominant red lettering across the top of the screen.

"God damn it," grimaced John, looking up at the computer system looming over him. "I guess that they're not going to make it that easy for me."

"Correct, Mister Bishop, we are not going to make it that easy for you."

Waves of fear, regret, and anger swelled within John's stomach as he instinctively turned his head towards the sound of the voice.

Standing calmly in front of the elevator doors with his arms across his chest, Mr. Smith glared at John from across the room with a look of disdain and unrestrained contempt.

"I always suspected that you were weak, Mister Bishop," spoke Mr. Smith, shaking his head back and forth. "You only made it halfway through your first list."

John held in place as Mr. Smith approached from between the two center rows of server towers.

"We took a chance with you, Mister Bishop, and you had so much potential," continued Mr. Smith. "I even thought that you could replace me one day, and I'm very disappointed to see that you've decided to turn your back on our agreement so quickly."

"How did you know?" muttered John, standing to face Mr. Smith.

"Does it matter, Mister Bishop?" questioned Mr. Smith as he continued to advance.

"Under the circumstances," replied John. "I think that it definitely matters."

"For new operators, the first six months with GENEPOL is a probationary period, Mister Bishop, and we've been monitoring your every movement since you decided to shake my hand," said Mr. Smith. "That is one speaking point that GENEPOL deliberately leaves out of our initial briefing."

John watched as Mr. Smith halted at the end of the computer servers, positioning himself directly between where John was standing and the elevator doors at the opposite side of the room.

"Don't look so surprised, Mister Bishop," spoke Mr. Smith, breaking the silence. "Do you remember when I said that you're not the first person that I've recruited?"

"I seem to remember you saying something about that," replied John.

"Well, Mister Bishop," said Mr. Smith, cinching his eyes at John. "You're also not the first operator that I've had to put down for having second thoughts."

John stared back at Mr. Smith, a sensation of overwhelming trepidation spreading throughout his body.

"Well, what happens now?" questioned John, looking down at the smart phone in his right hand.

"One of two things, Mister Bishop," answered Mr. Smith, placing his palm over his opposing fist. "We can either do this the intelligent way, or the incredibly painful way."

"That's exactly what I thought you were going to say," interjected John.

"If you have any sense of honor towards our agreement, or even a shred of common sense, Mister Bishop, you'll make this easy on both of us," spoke Mr. Smith, turning to raise his hand towards the elevator door. "Now please, come with me."

Silently wishing that he had spent more time thinking about contingency planning, John instinctively reacted with the first impulse that entered into his mind.

John swiftly raised his right arm and launched his smart phone upwards from his upstretched hand. Watching as Mr. Smith followed the rising cell phone with his eyes, John reached into his suit jacket to draw his pistol and then outstretched his arm. Flexing his grip around the trigger of the weapon, the pistol discharged to strike Mr. Smith in the torso, his body jolting backwards and collapsing down onto the floor as the gunshot echoed throughout the expanse of the room.

Lowering his pistol to his side, John reached out in front of his body to catch the falling cellular phone in the palm of his left hand.

John exhaled sharply and returned his pistol to the inside of his suit jacket. Grasping the smart phone in his hand, John instantly focused on why he was here and what he needed to do. Placing his phone gently into his left pant pocket, John turned towards the elevator door at the opposite side of the room and sprinted forward.

Crashing into the wall beside the elevator doors, John slammed his fist into the call button. Staring up at the floor indicator lights, John fought back a rush of panic by inhaling deeply. After a few moments the elevator opened, and John exhaled sharply as he stepped forward towards the doors.

"You never read the hand book did you, Mister Bishop?"

John froze, cautiously turning his head to see Mr. Smith standing upright in the same spot where he had been lying a few moments ago.

"If you'd have done what I told you and read the handbook, you'd have known that each of our suits contains a small lining of aramid fibres and provides a certain level of protection," said Mr. Smith as he moved towards John. "As such, there is just enough ballistic armour in each suit jacket to stop a round from a GENEPOL standard issue pistol."

John grimaced, lifting his arms away from his body to look down at his clothing.

"It's an innate security measure in the event that an operator makes the mistake of turning against us," continued Mr. Smith as he advanced down the centre rows of server towers. "So, Mister Bishop, that's exactly why I carry this around with me."

John held in place long enough to watch Mr. Smith reach into his jacket and draw a menacingly large calibre pistol before immediately turning back towards the elevator doors.

"Take one more step towards that door, Mister Bishop, and all of this will end right now," continued Mr. Smith, quickening his pace and raising his arm to speak down the barrel of his gun.

Gripped by frustration over the incredulous chain of events that had ultimately left him short of what he needed to do, John shook his head as the elevator doors mechanically closed in front of him. Turning to face Mr. Smith, John raised his arms and held up the palms of his hands.

"That's better, Mister Bishop," said Mr. Smith, halting as he emerged from between the computer servers. "Now, relinquish your side arm."

Mr. Smith motioned with the barrel of his pistol. Responding to the contentious prompt, John reached into his suit, carefully withdrew his pistol between his thumb and index finger, and then abruptly tossed the weapon onto the floor beside him.

"I'm not exactly sure what you were trying to accomplish, Mister Bishop," spoke Mr. Smith, glancing down at John's pistol lying on the floor. "But whatever you tried to steal from the Gene Police, I want it back."

Realizing that if he didn't immediately regain control of the situation he would end up as another statistic on Mr. Smith's power slideshow presentation, John slowly reached back into his suit jacket. Conscious to maintain a stoic demeanour, John placed the palm of his hand around a stun grenade carefully placed inside his jacket pocket and removed the safety clip with the tip of his index finger.

"Sure, Smith," said John, staring Mr. Smith directly in the eyes. "I've got what you're looking for right here."

Gently guiding the metallic pull ring away from the body of the grenade with his thumb, John shot his arm out in front of his body and released the device from the palm of his hand.

"MISTER BISHOP…" shouted Mr. Smith, his voice cut off by the bellow of a round discharging from his pistol.

Collapsing down onto the floor as the bullet pierced above his head, John shut his eyes and slapped his hands against his ears. The echo of the gunshot was immediately replaced by a concussive surge of intense heat and blazing light, and John opened his eyes to see Mr. Smith release a guttural roar and grasp at his face.

John rolled onto his stomach and thrust his arms and legs into the ground, launching his body and propelling himself forward. John twisted his torso and rammed his right shoulder into Mr. Smith, the force of the impact causing the agent to drop his pistol and fall backwards into the steel frame of the server tower. John reached with his left hand to grab Mr. Smith's shoulder, dropping his opposing hand to lash out with a blinding series of uppercuts.

"This was a mistake!" yelled John as he smashed his fist into Mr. Smith's rib cage. "This whole place is a horrible mistake!"

Dropping his right hand to his side, John reached out with a wide hook aimed at the side of Mr. Smith's head, and recovering faster than he would have thought possible, Mr. Smith dropped his body down to simultaneously duck under the incoming swing and jab his fist sharply into John's stomach. Unable to stop himself from doubling forward from the momentum of his failed attack and the blow to his midsection, John watched in his peripheral vision as Mr. Smith stepped forward and quickly pivoted to position himself directly behind him. John recoiled to his standing position and swung out with his right elbow, but his attack landed squarely into Mr. Smith's outstretched hand as he felt an arm reach over his left shoulder and firmly wrap itself around his throat.

"I fix mistakes for a living, Mister Bishop ," spoke Mr. Smith as he placed his right hand on the back of John's neck to tighten his hold. "The only mistake we've made was inviting you to join our order, a mistake which I intend to correct."

John reached up with both arms to claw at his neck, his breath cut off as Mr. Smith's forearm cinched pervasively around his throat. Attempting to center himself and stave off the panic from choking, John closed his eyes and lifted his arms over his head to grasp at Mr. Smith. Interlocking his fingers around the base of Mr. Smith's skull and focusing his remaining energy, John abruptly lowered his center of gravity and shot his torso forward to tear Mr. Smith overtop of his own body. A resounding thud echoed through the vast interior of the room, and John opened his eyes to see Mr. Smith lying outstretched on the floor directly in front of him.

Gasping for breath but realizing that he needed to retain the initiative, John shot his right fist downward to strike Mr. Smith firmly in the forehead and bounce his opponent's head cruelly off the tiled floor. John reached down to sharply grasp Mr. Smith's tie with both hands and then callously dragged the agent to his feet. Wrapping the neck tie tightly around his left hand and then pulling sharply, John watched Mr. Smith's persistent look of stoic resentment quickly dissipate into a baleful expression of rage, frustration, and fatigue.

"You're wrong Smith!" yelled John as he reached out with his right hand to strike Mr. Smith in the face. "You're wrong about me... you're wrong about everything and everyone... and I am here to stop this!"

John continued to lash out at Mr. Smith until a wave of exhaustion swelled up from his lungs and spread out over his body. Reaching out to grasp the base of Mr. Smith's tie with his right hand, John released a frenzied roar and swung his body around to drag the agent forward by the neck. John extended his arms outward and released his grip, planting his foot down to halt his momentum as Mr. Smith careened towards the elevator embedded into the adjacent wall.

Pulsing with adrenaline and choking for breath, John watched as Mr. Smith collided with the polished surface of the elevator doors before collapsing backwards onto the floor. Half expecting Mr. Smith to instantly resurrect himself and resume fighting, John held in place until he was confident that his opponent was finally incapacitated. Recovering his sidearm and then charging towards the elevator, John slammed his palm into the call button, hurtling forward into the enclosure as the elevator doors divided open.

"What am I doing and where the hell am I going!" spurted John, turning to face the string of numbered elevator call buttons.

While he had been allowed to enter the building without incident, John wasn't even sure if any additional security measures had been alerted to his intentions. John could try simply just walking out the front door, but if the security floor hadn't already been warned off then his battered appearance would have been enough to articulate to anyone that something was wrong. In the best case scenario, there were eight heavily armed guards standing watch over the only exit to the building, and all John was equipped to fight with was his pistol.

"I need a bigger gun," said John, staring down at the GENEPOL standard issue pistol in his hand. "There's a section of heavily armed soldiers down there and all I've got is... wait a minute."

The answer surged through John like a bolt of clairvoyance, and instantly he realized what he needed to do next.

"I need a bigger gun," repeated John as he reached out and tapped the button for the third floor of the building. "And we've got all the guns in the world right here."

One One

Remaining out of view as the doors opened, John took a furtive glance out over the GENEPOL training and load out centre. Grateful that the floor was deserted, John replaced his sidearm and advanced out of the elevator.

Racing to the far side of the room, John commenced a rampant but deliberate search of every locker, drawer, cabinet, and container on the floor, systematically working his way back towards the elevator. Finding only a vast array of stun guns, flash grenades, concealable melee weapons, and a number of tracking and surveillance devices, John looked out over the room with growing desperation.

"Unbelievable," spoke John as he held up two flash grenades before dropping them into his right pant pocket. "For an organization that specializes in population control, they seem to have a disproportionate amount of equipment that doesn't actually kill anyone."

John continued his frantic search until he reached an expansive steel cabinet sealed over by a metallic shutter. Reaching down to rip open the shutter, John was greeted by the sight of a rifle rack populated by an immaculate row of M4 carbine assault rifles and multiple well-ordered stacks of assorted ammunition lining the bottom of the enclosure.

"I knew it," said John, smiling and dropping his shoulders at the sight of the arsenal.

Raising his head to look at the upper section of the locker, John found himself staring up at an M249 light machine gun resting on the top shelf of the cabinet.

"To whatever God is listening," spoke John, reaching up to grab the machine gun by the carrying handle. "Thank you."

Lifting the ammunition feed tray and performing a hasty function test, John confirmed that the weapon had been prepped for firing and fully serviceable despite the lack of carbon on the interior or even the slightest sign of use. Satisfied with his new armament, John reached down and grabbed a single box of linked ammunition. Attaching the ammo box to the bottom of the machine gun, John laid the ammunition belt across the receiver, slammed the feed tray shut, and then pulled the cocking handle to chamber the first round.

"This definitely improves my odds," said John, looking up to survey the remainder of the room. "Let's see what else they've got."

John continued his hectic sweep across the floor of the training and load out centre, ignoring the desks, counters, and containers positioned in the middle of the room and focusing his search on the metal cabinets running along the wall. Progressing through each locker to find an impressive but nevertheless tactically infeasible collection of long range high precision rifles, lethal and non-lethal melee weapons, and an extensive row of GENEPOL standard issue black suits, John reached the final cabinet positioned beside the elevator. Wrenching the double doors to the locker open, John revealed a row of full body armor which bore a distinct resemblance to the tactical suits worn by the direct action response team.

"Oh hello, my old friend," spoke John, setting the machine gun down at his feet. "I am very, very glad to see you."

John dropped his shoulders and ripped the suit jacket from his body, grunting as he spun around to launch his jacket across the room.

"I won't need this anymore," said John, tearing the tie from his neck and undoing the top button of his shirt.

John reached into the locker, and beginning with his legs and working his way up, John systematically outfitted himself with the tactical body armor. Familiar with the suit from having worn a similar model several hundred times before, only a few moments elapsed before John was placing the helmet of the ballistic armor set onto his head.

"Perfect," spoke John, looking down over the form-fitting armor running across his body.

John reached down to shoulder the M249, and as he stepped towards the elevator a torrent of memories flooded into his mind. John couldn't help the feeling that all his time with the military, his years with the DART, and all of his previous experiences were suddenly culminating to help carry him through the next few moments. He had managed to steal the GENEPOL target list and even defeat Mr. Smith, something that he hadn't planned on doing or would have even thought possible, and there was only one final door to fight through in order to complete the most important mission of his entire life.

"Who knows, John, maybe you'll discover the cure for cancer as well," said John as he slammed his fist into the elevator call button. "Then all of this will just be another exciting chapter in your memoires."

The elevator sprang open and John advanced inside, pressing the button for the first floor and causing the doors to seal behind him. As the elevator began to descend, John reached down and removed the two flash grenades from his right pocket. John quickly removed the safety clip from each grenade, strapping one grenade to his tactical vest and then firmly gripping the other in his left hand as he gently removed the pin. Lowering the protective shield on his helmet down over his face, John pressed his back against the wall of the elevator, held the grenade out in front of his body, and looked up to watch the floor indicator light flash to the far left-hand position.

"Go on the ding," said John, commanding himself not to hesitate.

The elevator became still and resonated a familiar chime, and as the elevator doors divided, John reached out and hurled the flash grenade out through the opening. John hastily returned to his cover position behind the wall of the elevator, and there was a moment of silence indicating that he had been fortunate enough to catch GENEPOL's local security off guard.

"GRENADE!" bellowed a male voice from the security floor.

There was a fury of commotion accented by a series of panicked yells, but the upheaval was immediately cut off as a blinding pulse of light seared through the confines of the GENEPOL security station. John stepped between the elevator doors to see four security guards and one bystander plain clothes staff officer laying strewn across the floor in varying states of agony. Raising his machine gun to waist level, John laid on the trigger of his M249 to send a torrent of bullets raining out over the floor.

John didn't need to kill the guards in order to escape the building, but he definitely needed to supress them, and the four guards on the opposite side of the entrance shielded behind the metal wall dividing the room represented the greatest threat. Firing burst after burst from the machine gun, John began to focus his fire on the doorway and the flashes of movement on the opposite side of the room as he advanced.

"LOCK IT DOWN!" yelled a voice from the far side of the door.

An alarm siren blasted out into the room to couple with the incessant cry of gunfire, and John could see the steel barrier hanging over the security door begin to descend. Realizing that he had to act immediately to avoid being trapped inside the building, John tore the remaining flash grenade from his tactical vest and lobbed the grenade through the door, and against his better judgement, John leaped forward to follow the path of the grenade. Hugging the M249 to his chest, John landed on his knees to slide forward underneath the plunging steel barricade.

Collapsing down onto his back, John was engulfed by a hail of bullets and he could feel the unmistakable kinetic sting of rounds striking him in the torso as a barrage of ricochets consumed the floor around him. The stream of panicked fire continued for only a fraction of a second before the room was engulfed by a cataclysmic reverberation followed by instant silence.

Unsure if he was alive, dying, or dead, John was uniquely grateful for the rising sound of the security alarm as his hearing slowly returned. John lifted his face shield and sat up from the floor to see two GENEPOL security guards lying passively on the ground to his left, a third guard to his right babbling incoherently as he rocked his head back and forth, and a fourth guard standing to his front crushing his fists into his eyes. Drawing on his remaining adrenaline, John pushed himself up off the ground and charged forward, striking the remaining standing guard with the butt of his machine gun and knocking the man to the floor. John stumbled across the room to the service elevator, rammed the palm of his hand into the call button, and then turned to address the room.

"I don't have time to figure out which one of you shot me," spoke John, wincing as he ran his hand over the bullet marks lining his body armor. "But if you have any sense of self-preservation you will STAY ON THE GROUND UNTIL I LEAVE!"

The service elevator sounded and the doors parted open, and John held in place to dissuade any final acts of reciprocity from the four disoriented security guards before stepping backwards into the elevator. John reached over and pressed the button for the parking garage, removing his helmet and tossing it down onto the security floor as the service elevator doors sealed shut.

"Almost done, John... almost done," spoke John as he rubbed away the sweat collecting on his forehead. "Now let's get out of here and end this."

John took a step backwards and adopted a firing position, raising the M249 to his shoulder as the elevator decelerated. The elevator chimed and the doors parted open to reveal a refined but very startled young woman staring back at John through the sights of the machine gun. Making a downward patting motion with his hand in the air, John waited for the woman to drop to her knees and raise her hands before relaxing his finger off the trigger.

Although he didn't recognize the woman, John was reasonably certain from her conservative blue business suit and apprehensive demeanor that she wasn't an operator.

"It's a good thing that you didn't decide to wear black to work today, ma'am," said John, letting the barrel of the M249 drop towards the floor. "Otherwise I probably would have shot you in the face."

Holding his palm in the air to indicate that he meant no harm, John stepped out of the service elevator and cautiously advanced past the woman before sprinting forward. John raced across the floor of the parkade, dodging through identical rows of black sedans to reach his vehicle.

Ripping open the door to his car, John threw the M249 into the passenger seat of the vehicle, dropped himself into the driver's seat, and slammed the door closed behind him. John simultaneously twisted the keys positioned in the ignition and slammed his foot down on the accelerator, wrenching the gear shift into drive as the vehicle jerked forward.

Pressed back into his seat by the ensuing acceleration, John gripped the steering wheel and rapidly negated the vehicle through the matching rows of black sedans lining the confines of the parking garage towards the narrow exit tunnel. The front end frame of the vehicle collided with the incline of the concrete exit ramp, and John jarred forward as he pinned his foot down onto the accelerator and ascended upwards.

John exhaled sharply as he crested the exit of the parking garage and ploughed forward into the darkened city street. The listless calm of the downtown night sky remained only for a moment before John was enveloped by a ubiquitous blinding light. Using one hand to shield his eyes and the other to wrench the steering wheel to the left, John slammed his foot on the brake to bring the vehicle to a skidding halt. John's eyes focused on the light and he could make out more than two dozen headlights arrayed in a semi-circle around the front of the building, and simultaneously exiting the driver's side of each vehicle was a man or woman dressed in a black suit and tie.

"Oh my God," spoke John, crushing the steering wheel with his hands. "This wasn't supposed to happen."

John looked out the window at the underground parking entrance to GENEPOL headquarters, then out over the undivided line of vehicles swarmed around him, and then down at the M249 laying on the passenger seat beside him. John slapped the gear shift into park and grabbed the machine gun, kicking open the driver side door and then lunging into a kneeling position against the trunk of his vehicle. Reacting as if they had collectively rehearsed a response, each operator standing along the blockade of vehicles hastily reached into their suit jackets to withdraw a GENEPOL standard issued pistol.

Encircled by twenty nine outstretched pistols all aimed in his direction, John let of a low growl and then shook his head.

"I was so close," said John, reaching down to touch the smart phone in his left pocket. "At least I will have the satisfaction of taking a few of these psychopaths with me."

"That's enough, Mister Bishop!" commanded a voice from behind John.

Removing his hand from his pocket and gripping the stock of the machine gun, John turned his head to see Mr. Smith staggering up the parkade entrance holding his pistol in his outstretched hand.

Before he could swing the barrel of the light machine gun the sound of a gunshot pierced the still of the city street, and John felt the rush of a bullet sear past his head and imbed itself into the trunk of his vehicle. John froze, silently waiting for the sound of a second gun shot to tear his life away.

"I was reasonably certain that I could beat you, Mister Bishop," spoke Mr. Smith, speaking over the barrel of his gun as he limped forward. "But as you can see for yourself, by no means overconfident."

John glanced over the trunk of the car at the row of stoic GENEPOL operators and then back at Mr. Smith. Taking a small amount of silent satisfaction that it took GENEPOL in its entirety to stop him, John stood up, dropped the M249 light machine gun onto the pavement beside him, and then turned to face the sound of the approaching footsteps.

Holding in place with his hands at his sides, John watched as Mr. Smith casually passed the barrel of his pistol into the palm of his opposing hand and then lunged forward, lashing out with his arm to smash the butt of his heavy set pistol into the side of John's head. John's vision vaporized into a field of black as he collapsed down onto the asphalt street, his consciousness returning to see Mr. Smith's foot sail forward and strike him in the chest.

"You've caused me more trouble then you were ever worth!" growled Mr. Smith as he repeatedly rammed his foot into John's torso. "It takes a lot to make me angry, and I am going to make you bleed for all the damage you've done!"

Mr. Smith took a step back and inhaled deeply, reaching up to adjust his tie.

"The data you stole, Mister Bishop," demanded Mr. Smith, pointing his pistol directly into John's face. "Give it to me... now!"

"Alright, Smith," choked John as he rolled over onto his back. "You win."

Wincing as he pressed himself off the ground, John summoned his remaining energy to stand and face Mr. Smith. John reached down into his left pocket and carefully removed his smart phone. Cradling the device in his hands, John tapped the screen of the phone once with his finger, smiling back at the electronic glow radiating up from the screen.

"Here you go, Smith," said John, extending his arm up to Mr. Smith. "For the good of all mankind."

Mr. Smith cinched his eyes with obvious apprehension, reaching out to take the phone from John's hand before examining the screen.

"My God, John," spoke Mr. Smith, his eyes transfixed on the phone. "What have you done?"

Mr. Smith watched impassively as a data transfer progress bar rapidly expanded across the screen and then vanished to reveal an electronic message entitled "The Gene Police Are Real" addressed to every newspaper, radio station, social media outlet, and television broadcast station in the city.

Epilogue

"Television on, ascending ten second preview, all channels."

"Acknowledged, channel one."

"Rioting continued throughout the downtown core for the fifth consecutive day. Reporting remains sporadic, but the list of casualties and injuries continues to escalate with property damage estimated in the hundreds of millions. An additional division of regular force military personnel arrived today to assist police in regaining control over the city streets and restoring essential services. Thousands of arrests have already been made, and the perpetrators appear as diverse as the city itself as the dusk till dawn curfew continues."

"Channel two."

"I can't believe this is happening. This is total anarchy. Today I help my dad spray paint the words there's nothing left on the front lawn of our home. All our windows are smashed, and looters have taken everything. The sad part is that it could be worse, and all that's of the house across the street is a burnt out concrete hole. I've started to see the police again, but after what's happened I'm not sure who to trust… where are good people supposed to go?"

"Channel three."

"Super-sized, fun sized, or gigantized! What's that gonna cost you!?! Buy one get one free at Burger Master! With only thirty-seven grams of fat, our..."

"Next channel."

"Acknowledged, channel four."

"I swear to all of you that I knew nothing about the existence of this secret organization. But mark my words, this administration will personally spearhead the federal investigation to find the people responsible, the so called Gene Police, concurrent to employing whatever force is necessary to restore order and safeguard the civil liberties of each and every constituent of this great nation."

"Channel five."

"I've been a reporter for twelve years, and I get a lot of leads thrown at me, some good, some completely insane. At first I thought it was the ramblings of a paranoid schizophrenic who checks the back seat of his car every time he gets inside, but it didn't take me long to figure out that half of the people on the list were already dead, and some of the names had been reported missing even after the message had been sent out. I still have no idea who or what the Gene Police are, but someone was killing these people. I feel terrible about everything that's happened, but the list was sent out to most of the journalists in the city. If I didn't figure it out, then someone else from the media…"

"Channel six."

"The demons! The demons my children! The demons walk among us! They have been here all along, and it was only a matter of time until they made themselves known. Do not let the anarchy or confusion grip you, as that is the path of deception where the devil will lead you! At the end of the world, at the end of time, at the end of days, all you need to know is that the Lord is your shepherd, the only shepherd who can guide us, and he shall see the faithful through this dark awakening. Believe. Believe! Believe my children! Believe in the Lord and you shall be…"

"Next channel!"

"Acknowledged, channel seven."

"Tracing the digital origin of the message to the initial cell phone relay tower, a search of the surrounding area has revealed only an abandoned building. There is still no sign or follow on communication from John Bishop, the man responsible for sending the original message. With no indication of his whereabouts, we are left with only speculation behind Mister Bishop's motives. Is he a hero, a villain, or an unsung martyr responsible for uncovering a malicious government conspiracy?"

"STOP!" yelled Mr. Smith, jolting forward in his chair. "Television off."

"Thank you for using Teleview, and good night," answered the obtuse electronic female voice as the television flashed to darkness.

"God damn you Bishop, you're responsible for all of this," said Mr. Smith, crushing his fists together. "I suppose everyone thinks that you're the hero."

The cellular phone on the adjoining end table erupted, and Mr. Smith snatched his hand down onto the device and then held the phone up to his ear.

"Romans," spoke a gentle female voice. "Please authenticate."

"Thirteen four," responded Mr. Smith.

"Confirmed," continued the female voice. "Please wait one."

The phone emitted a rustling of movement, and the soft female voice was replaced by a man with a harsh direct tone.

"One one, this is niner," spoke the man. "Have you been watching the news?

"Yes," answered Mr. Smith. "I've tried to never underestimate the power of human stupidity, but this goes far beyond anything I would have expected."

"I know, it's a real mess," answered the man. "I'm taking it that you managed to get clear?"

"My new accommodations leave a lot to be desired," said Mr. Smith, rolling his eyes over the worn down interior of the motel room. "But I have everything that I need."

"We cleaned out the home base before we left," continued the man. "However, until we can confirm what they know about us, if anything, I would stay well away from your home."

"Have you heard anything from zero higher?" questioned Mr. Smith, looking back over at the television.

"That's the thing, even though they've publicly denounced us, there's been no official order," said the man. "I know they're busy, but just like before, I take their silence as implied consent to continue the work."

"What about the other shepherds?" asked Mr. Smith.

"We're completely reliant on unsecure means, and we're having difficultly contacting anyone," answered the man. "Most have likely disappeared and gone into hiding."

"I suppose we can't blame them," said Mr. Smith. "It is almost impossible to mitigate something like this."

"Have you had a chance to look at your to do list?" asked the man on the phone.

"I've just returned from the post office," responded Mr. Smith, reaching over to lift up a file folder positioned on the adjacent table.

"We were able to move the tower, but it's in a thousand pieces right now," spoke the man. "Trying to assemble the infrastructure required to operate a supercomputer would draw attention that we definitely need to avoid."

"How have you been collecting files?" asked Mr. Smith.

"We've started with the emergency response network," said the man. "This particular file has made fourteen withdrawals from the food bank over the last five days."

"He seems a little overweight for someone who is supposedly starving," said Mr. Smith, dropping the folder back down on the table. "If the address is current, he will be prosecuted in approximately thirty-seven minutes."

"There is no rush, one one, and take as much time as you need to avoid detection," answered the man on the telephone. "Although there are too many to go after all at once, the rioting has been the perfect time to start taking down names, and even without the tower we've managed to compile multiple entries for subsequent to do lists."

"Anything interesting?" questioned Mr. Smith.

"Multiple gang members, a laundry list of outstanding warrants for ongoing looting, robberies, and willful destruction, and even a corrupt construction firm owner who conveniently raised the price of his services seven fold in the last-few days," continued the man, speaking as if he was reading from a prepared text.

"Good," responded Mr. Smith. "I've always enjoyed putting an end to those who try to take advantage of others."

"One other thing," continued the man. "I'm sorry to say this, but we've had to reallocate all funding to our off-shore accounts to avoid detection and seizure, and you'll have to survive of whatever you have squirreled away."

"That's fine," responded Mr. Smith. "I don't anticipate retiring any time soon."

"As of right now, you're one of the few we have left," spoke the voice on the phone. "Despite all that's going on, I'm certain you know what will happen if pseudo morality and idealistic ideology continues unabated."

"As much as it troubles me to say, I'd like to believe that the human race is still worth saving," responded Mr. Smith.

"The irony is that history may never really appreciate all the work that we've done."

"History will absolve all of us, but there may be no one left to interpret the past if we don't continue to define who controls the future," answered the man. "For the good of all mankind, one one, and good luck."

"One one acknowledges all," said Mr. Smith.

The phone went silent, and Mr. Smith dropped the cell phone into his jacket pocket. Picking up the file folder from the table beside his chair, Mr. Smith moved to a small lock box embedded into the motel closet wall. After inputting a seven digit code the door to the wall safe sprung open, and Mr. Smith reached into the steel enclosure to exchange the file folder for a black heavy calibre pistol before sealing the safe door.

Mr. Smith cocked the action on his sidearm, holstered the pistol inside his suit jacket, and then crossed over towards the door of the motel room. Reaching out to twist the handle, Mr. Smith pulled opened the door as the sound of sirens, sporadic gunfire, and distant unabated anarchy washed over him.

"For the good of all mankind," spoke Mr. Smith, advancing through the entrance of the motel and slamming the door behind him.